**The man was nothing but trouble…
but he sure could kiss!**

Before she had time to protest, he had kissed her, threading his fingers through her hair so she couldn't pull away.

Not that she tried. Not for a moment or two at least..

What she did was part her lips and melt into the kiss. The joining tasted like ambrosia, his scent making her crave him even more. His kiss was warm, soft and inviting, and when he slid a hand down her arm to curve around her waist—

She stepped back and gave him a good slap.

Cage looked stunned. "What did you do that for?"

"You don't just come to a woman's room and assume you'll be welcome. Next time, you ask first."

"Next time—"

She grabbed his shirt and pulled him all the way into the room.

AMANDA STEVENS

SHOWDOWN *in* WEST TEXAS

TORONTO • NEW YORK • LONDON
AMSTERDAM • PARIS • SYDNEY • HAMBURG
STOCKHOLM • ATHENS • TOKYO • MILAN • MADRID
PRAGUE • WARSAW • BUDAPEST • AUCKLAND

Recycling programs
for this product may
not exist in your area.

ISBN-13: 978-0-373-88917-4

SHOWDOWN IN WEST TEXAS

This edition published by arrangement with Harlequin Books S.A.

® and TM are trademarks of the publisher. Trademarks indicated with
® are registered in the United States Patent and Trademark Office, the
Canadian Trade Marks Office and in other countries.

www.eHarlequin.com

Printed in U.S.A.

ABOUT THE AUTHOR

Amanda Stevens is a bestselling author of more than thirty novels of romantic suspense. In addition to being a Romance Writers of America RITA® Award finalist, she is also a recipient of awards for Career Acheivement in Romantic/Mystery and Career Acheivement in Romantic/Suspense from *Romantic Times BOOKreviews* magazine. She currently resides in Texas. To find out more about past, present and future projects, please visit her Web site at www.amandastevens.com.

Books by Amanda Stevens

Don't miss any of our special offers. Write to us at the following address for information on our newest releases.

Harlequin Reader Service
U.S.: 3010 Walden Ave., P.O. Box 1325, Buffalo, NY 14269
Canadian: P.O. Box 609, Fort Erie, Ont. L2A 5X3

CAST OF CHARACTERS

Cage Nichols—A down-on-his-luck salesman witnesses a brutal shootout, assumes the identity of a hit man, poses as a hotshot detective and falls for the new sheriff. And that's just Day One.

Sheriff Grace Steele—Someone wants her dead, and the new guy just wants her. She can handle the drug smugglers, the dirty cops, a conniving ex-husband and her disgruntled little sister, but love is like West Texas…not for the faint of heart.

Detective Lily Steele—For years she's carried a grudge against her big sister. Now that Grace is back in Jericho Pass, Lily thinks it's time for a showdown.

Colt McKinney—A wheeler-dealer known as the Donald Trump of Cochise County. Did he have an ulterior motive for bringing Grace back to Jericho Pass?

Jesse Nance—Grace's ex-husband has a little deed problem. And a great big secret.

Sookie Truesdale—Jesse's new live-in is manipulative, greedy and high maintenance. And those are her good qualities.

Ethan Brennan—A mild-mannered tenderfoot with a not-so-secret crush.

Dale Walsh—Hit man? Cop? Or both?

Chapter One

"Lily is absolutely livid." Grace Steele adjusted the headset of her cell phone so that her fingers were free to drum impatiently on the steering wheel. "I don't know that she'll ever forgive me. If she could find a way to do me in without getting caught, I think she might actually try it."

"I'm assuming that's a gross exaggeration," Colt McKinney said from the other end. "Although, I don't doubt she'll get a secret kick out of making your life miserable for a while."

"Nothing secret about it," Grace said. "She'll revel in it."

"Have you tried reasoning with her?"

"Have you?"

Grace heard his easygoing chuckle through the earpiece, and she wished they could share a good laugh the way they used to back in high school. But it had been a long time since she'd found life even remotely amusing, and she wasn't at all confident that things would be looking up any time soon.

However, if anyone could put the semblance of a smile on her face, it was Colt. He was as charming and handsome as ever, but Grace had never thought of him as anything more than a good friend. Now that they were professional associates, it was important to her that they not allow even so much as a hint of impropriety to taint their relationship. The last thing she needed was to be accused of sleeping her way to the top.

Again.

Colt McKinney was one of four elected commissioners that governed Cochise County, and was personally responsible for bringing Grace back to Jericho Pass to serve as the interim sheriff while Charlie Dickerson underwent treatment for throat cancer.

If someone had told Grace this time last year that she'd be returning to her hometown—a place she'd left without a backward glance after high school—she'd have laughed in their face. Only a few months ago, she'd still been a rising star in the prestigious TBI—Texas Bureau of Investigation.

But a botched case and a dead agent had placed Grace squarely on the wrong side of a review board, and she'd soon discovered just how quickly her fortunes could change when her superior—who also happened to be her lover—needed a way to save his own hide.

She'd been suspended without pay pending an internal investigation, and when termination seemed inevitable, she'd decided to salvage what little she had left of her pride and her professional integrity by tendering her resignation. Colt's offer had come at a time when she'd desperately needed a graceful exit from Austin, and she'd latched on with both hands.

Unfortunately, her arrival in Jericho Pass hadn't exactly been met without controversy or resentment, either. There were those in the Cochise County Sheriff's office who had felt—and still did—that the selection should have come from within the department. That Colt, in fact, was playing favoritism by appointing an old friend to the position.

But in light of recent intelligence reports and an uptick in violence along the border, he and the other commissioners had been determined to bring in someone with Grace's training and experience, not to mention her political connections at the state capital.

Because of its proximity to the border, Jericho Pass sat in a particularly vulnerable location. The good-old-boy network that had run things for years in Cochise County was no longer sufficient to combat the narco-traffickers who were often armed with better technology and weaponry than the police.

"We knew there'd be some hard feelings in the department when we brought you in," Colt said. "But it's only been a few weeks. Give it some time. They'll come around."

"Lily won't."

"You sound pretty sure about that."

"I know my sister."

"Then what do you propose we do?"

"Nothing. I'm not leaving Jericho Pass with my tail tucked between my legs just because my little sister can't get past our old sibling rivalry." Grace simultaneously gripped the steering wheel and pressed down on the gas. She had the road to herself, and when the powerful V-8 engine kicked in, her truck shot down the road like a rocket. "I came here to do a job and I intend to do it."

"Good for you."

"But that doesn't mean I can't give Lily some space," she said. "I'm moving out of the ranch house today. I must have been out of my mind, thinking we could live together without one of us killing the other."

"Things are that bad, huh?"

"Worse. But I'm used to it."

"Where will you go?"

"I've taken a room at Miss Nelda's until I can find a place of my own in town."

"Well, hang in there," Colt said. "Tempers are bound to be on edge, what with the department being so shorthanded and all. But with you at the helm, and now with the possibility of a new deputy coming on board, things should ease up."

"I've been meaning to talk to you about that. Have you met this guy?"

"You mean Dale Walsh? Not in person, no, but he comes highly recommended. Charlie's been trying to get him out here for an interview ever since they met at the Homeland Security Conference in San Antonio. And I trust Charlie's judgment. He may not have your pedigree in law enforcement, but he knows people."

"When Walsh eventually shows up, I'll let you know what I think," Grace said noncommittally.

"Fair enough. In the meantime, if you need anything, you just give us a holler, okay? I want you to be happy here, Grace. If Charlie decides not to come back—"

Grace wasn't about to make any promises. Not yet, at least. "Let's just cross that bridge when and if we get to it, okay? Listen, you're starting to break up. I'll talk to you when I get back to town."

She was coming upon the cutoff, and Grace removed her earpiece and tossed it onto the seat beside her as she automatically turned on her blinker, though there was no one else around for miles. Once she left the highway behind, the truck tires kicked up a dust cloud so thick, she could see nothing in the rearview mirror but a swirl of brown grit. Ahead of her, only the vast nothingness of the West Texas landscape—blue sky, desert and the eerie silhouette of the distant rock mesas.

Grace had been gone from the area for so many years, she'd forgotten how exposed and insignificant one could feel in such a limitless landscape. How the fragile quality of the light seemed to echo the transient nature of man's footprint here in this infinite wasteland, this last frontier.

She slowed as she drove through the high arches that welcomed visitors to the Steele ranch. Grace had lived happily on that spread with her parents and her two sisters for the first ten years of her life. Then her mother and father had been murdered in their sleep one night, and Grace's grandmother had moved down from Midland to raise her and her sisters. The killer had never been apprehended, and the lack of justice for their slain parents had led all three women into law enforcement, albeit down very different paths.

Rachel, the oldest, had gone off to study psychology at Tulane. After earning her graduate degree, she'd been recruited by the FBI into one of the Behavioral Analysis Units.

Grace had left town five years later to pursue a degree in Criminal Justice with a concentration in Forensic Science at the University of Texas at San Antonio. She'd spent seven years with the Austin Police Department before joining the TBI.

Lily was the only sister who had remained in Jericho Pass. After attending the local community college, she'd been hired on as first a dispatcher, then a patrol officer with the Cochise County Sheriff's Department. She was now one of three deputies—soon to be four, if Dale Walsh worked out—who made up Criminal Investigations.

Grace had learned through the grapevine—aka Miss Nelda and her sister, Georgina—that Lily had had her eye on the interim position ever since Charlie Dickerson had made public his diagnosis. She'd made no bones about her intention to run for sheriff, in spite of her age, if he decided to retire after his treatment. A temporary stint in the office would have given her a leg up on her opponents, but her sister's unexpected return had squelched her big plans.

Grace could sympathize with Lily's disappointment over the way things had turned out. Grace had had her share of setbacks, too. But even if she'd declined the position, Lily was never going to be appointed. Colt had told her as much. Lily didn't have enough experience or formal training to deal with the challenges along the border these days. At least this way, Grace could take her sister under her wing and help season her, if Lily would allow it.

That was a big *if*.

Lily's frustration, and to a certain extent her resentment, was understandable, but her simmering hostility was something Grace still did not get. What had she done to make Lily dislike her so intensely?

The dust cloud followed Grace around the

circular drive, and she waited for it to settle before she climbed out of the truck and stood for a moment, gazing up at the house.

Built out of limestone, it was two stories with screened-in porches on the front and back where Grace used to sit on summer nights and watch the stars with her father. The only sound, save for the hush of her father's voice as he pointed out the constellations, was the creaking of the windmill. Even now, that sound was one of Grace's most vivid memories.

It was the creaking of the windmill that had awakened her that night.

AFTER THE FUNERALS, Grandma Stella had moved the girls into a tiny rental house in town. The change of scenery had probably been the best thing for them at the time, but after a while, it seemed more practical to return to the ranch where they could all have their space.

Some of the neighbors had come over and cleaned up the place. They'd aired out all the rooms, shampooed the rugs and even went so far as to add a fresh coat of paint here and there. But no amount of paint or primer could eliminate the horror of what had happened upstairs. Nothing could ease such a tragic loss except the passage of enough time.

Eventually, the ranch had come to seem like home again, but it was a long time before Grace had been able to be by herself in the house. And no wonder. She and Lily had been there when it happened.

Grace still remembered the exact time when the windmill had awakened her. She knew because she'd glanced at the clock radio on the nightstand between her and Lily's beds. Throwing back the covers, she'd started to climb out of bed and pad over to the window to stare up at the night sky when another sound registered. Someone was coming up the stairs. Grace wanted to believe the cautious footfalls belonged to one of her parents, or maybe Rachel had come home early from her sleepover.

But something about those footsteps…

About the long hesitation at the top of the stairs…

Looking back, Grace was never sure what had alerted her to danger, but for some reason, she slipped out of bed and shook her sister awake. Then with a fingertip to her lips, she dragged Lily onto the floor and shoved her under the bed where the two of them cowered as the footsteps came closer.

The sound stilled again at the open door of the girls' bedroom, just long enough for Grace to catch a fleeting glimpse of dark boots— nothing more—before the footfalls continued down the hallway to her parents' bedroom.

If she'd called out a warning, would she have frightened the killer away? Or would she and Lily have met with the same fate as their parents?

There was no way of knowing, of course. And if she'd learned anything in the twenty-three years since that night, it was that guilt couldn't change a damn thing about the past, but it could sure play hell with the present.

Using the key Lily had begrudgingly given her, Grace let herself into the quiet house. Since their grandmother had died, her sister had been living there all alone.

I couldn't do it.

Even after all these years, Grace still didn't like being alone in that house.

I'm not as brave as Lily, she thought as she climbed the stairs.

The door to her and her sister's old bedroom was ajar, and Grace couldn't resist peeking in. She knew she should respect her sister's privacy, but curiosity got the better of her. Lily had been so careful about keeping that door closed, about shutting Grace out from the space they'd once shared, that the room had become almost symbolic of the barrier she'd erected between them.

She knocked on the door. "Lily, you in there?"

Her sister's truck hadn't been in the driveway, but she could have pulled around back to park.

Grace pushed the door open a little wider. The scent of her sister's perfume—a floral scent with a woodsy undertone—drifted out.

"I just came back to pack up my things. I'll be out of your hair in no time."

Grace stood on the threshold and glanced around. Gone were the pink ruffles from their childhood and the rock-band posters from their adolescence. Lily had redone the room in a sophisticated palette of beige and grayish blue. Gone, too, were the canopied twin beds with matching coverlets and piles of pillows. In their place was a spacious queen-size with chic but minimalist bedding.

The room could have come straight from Grace's townhouse in Austin. The sleek, urban furnishings seemed much more in keeping with her taste than Lily's. Her sister had always been such a romantic. But then, what did she really know about Lily these days? They hadn't been truly close since they were kids.

Regret tightened Grace's chest as she backed out the door. She'd been staying in Rachel's old bedroom since her return, and she hurried there now to pack up her things. As she fastened the lid on her last suitcase, she heard the squeak of a door and went out into the hallway to see if her sister had come in.

"Lily?"

Grace went to the top of the stairs and peered over the railing. "Lily, is that you?"

No answer.

She went back to Rachel's room, grabbed the suitcases and carried them down the hallway.

As she approached the landing, she heard another sound, this time from Lily's room.

Or so she thought.

As Grace started to turn, she caught a blur of movement out of the corner of her eye a split second before something hit her from behind.

Her bags tumbled down the stairs as she tried to grab hold of the banister to check her fall.

But it was too late. Already, she was plunging headlong down the wooden staircase.

When she hit the bottom, she rolled onto

her back, so dazed she couldn't immediately process what had happened. Nor did she feel any pain.

In the space of a heartbeat, the only thing that registered was a face at the top of the stairs, peering down at her.

Chapter Two

As Cage Nichols watched the cloud of steam mushroom over the hood of his car, he was reminded of his mother's favorite saying: "Son, if we didn't have bad luck, we wouldn't have no luck at all."

Back then, Cage hadn't entirely subscribed to Darleen's pessimistic outlook on life. Sure, they'd seen a lot of hard times after the old man took off, but Cage had been a good-looking, popular kid with a talent for football and girls, and he'd never minded hard work. Growing up in a small East Texas town, he hadn't needed much else.

But out in the real world, he'd discovered soon enough that a man needed more than looks and gumption to get by. Even a good education and the right connections could only take him so far. What a man really had to have was a little luck.

Cage could remember the exact moment when his had run out—at precisely 9:56 on a Friday night sixteen years ago.

He'd caught the winning touchdown in the last game of the season just as the clock wound down. In that moment of mindless exhilaration, he'd failed to note the two-hundred-and-fifty-pound linebacker still bearing down on him from his left. The late hit had caught him completely off guard, and the resulting knee injury had ended his dream of a full-ride scholarship to Southern Methodist University.

Ten years later, a hollow-nose bullet fired at close range from a thug's 9mm handgun into the same knee had ended his career as a SWAT officer with the Dallas P.D.

Now Cage sold oilfield equipment for his brother-in-law, Wayne Cordell. Or tried to.

His sales record had been pretty dismal thus far, partly because of the downturn in the economy, but mostly because Cage wasn't much of a salesman.

Which was why he desperately needed to close the El Paso deal.

Which was why the steam pouring out of the grill of his car as he coasted to the shoulder of the road made him want to put his fist through the windshield.

Instead, he got out, raised the hood, then slammed it shut a few minutes later. Just his luck. He'd blown a damn radiator hose.

Helluva place to be stranded, he thought, as he took stock of his surroundings. He was literally in the middle of nowhere. A good hundred and eighty miles from El Paso and less than twenty miles from the Mexican border. A no-man's-land of tumbleweed, cholla cactus, and whatever wildlife could survive the blistering Chihuahuan Desert heat.

Sweat trickled down Cage's back as he got out his phone and checked for a signal. *Nada.*

Well, that figured.

What aggravated him more than the inconvenience of the breakdown was Wayne's warning before Cage left Dallas. "That clunker won't get you as far as Waco, much less El Paso. Just fly down there tomorrow, close the deal, and get your ass back here with that contract. Or else don't bother coming back at all," he'd added with an ominous glare.

If Cage had followed his brother-in-law's advice, he'd already be in El Paso working on his pitch for the four o'clock meeting. Afterward, he could have hopped on a Southwest Airlines jet and been back home in time for the Mavericks tip-off since they were playing on the West Coast that night.

But, no.

Cage had had the bright idea to drive down overnight, drop in on a few of their best customers and hope that the personal touch and a little charm might persuade them to throw a couple of bones his way.

But that hadn't exactly worked out like gangbusters. Mostly, it had been a big waste of time.

So, not only would he end up getting canned for blowing the El Paso deal, he'd have to listen to Wayne's *I told you so* from now until eternity—or until his sister wised up and divorced the smug bastard.

Not that Cage was in any position to cast stones. He was hardly a catch himself these days. And if he hadn't been so damn hardheaded, he wouldn't be in his current predicament—miles off the beaten track, stuck in the desert with a half-empty water bottle and a dead cell phone to his name.

Things are really looking up for you, buddy.

He tried to find the bright side as he watched an earless lizard peeking through the orange blossoms of a prickly pear. At least he wasn't that far from the nearest town. He'd seen a sign a few miles back for a place called San Miguel.

But when Cage got out his map, he couldn't find it in the listings. Probably one of those tiny outposts along the Mexican border that time and civilization had forsaken.

He was doubtful he'd find a garage there, but surely he'd be able to use a landline to call for a tow truck…from somewhere. At the very least, he could let the El Paso folks know he'd likely be later than four.

He glanced at his watch. High noon. With any luck—and he'd be a fool to count on that—he could be up and running by two, and if he put the pedal to the metal, he might still make El Paso by five, with just enough time to close the deal and keep Wayne off his back.

Wishful thinking, but what else did he have going for him at the moment?

Grabbing the water bottle from the car, Cage tucked the folded map in his back pocket and struck out on foot. The desert was like an oven this time of day, and his shirt and hair were soon soaked with sweat.

He could feel the hot pavement burning through his boots, and the sight of a rattler sunning itself on the side of the road didn't exactly improve his mood, nor did the circling buzzards overhead. He ignored the vultures and gave the snoozing snake a wide berth as he kept on walking.

By the time he arrived in San Miguel, a grimy little settlement of crumbling brick buildings and faded adobe houses, the blistering heat had sapped his energy and his bum knee felt as if someone had punched red-hot needles through the muscles.

As he hobbled down the baking sidewalk, Cage took note of the businesses—a pawn shop, a pool hall, a boarded-up gas station, two churches and up ahead, a post office, judging by the flags waving overhead. But no garage.

The main thoroughfare through town was paved, but dust swirled up like a cyclone as a black SUV with tinted windows sped by him. It was a late-model vehicle and expensive. Cage wondered what it was doing way out here in the middle of nowhere. But then, whoever was behind those tinted windows could be thinking the same thing about him.

An old red pickup truck pulled to the curb in front of the post office, and an attractive blonde in tight jeans and a pink T-shirt hopped out of the cab. Her hair was pulled back in a ponytail, highlighting her smooth, tanned complexion and the shimmering lip gloss that was the exact shade of her shirt.

She was young, but not so young that her lingering glance made Cage uneasy. She was probably in her early to midtwenties. Fair game if he'd been in the mood.

"Excuse me," he said as he limped toward her.

"Well, hello." She planted a hand on her blue-jeaned hip as she gave him an interested perusal. "Where did you come from, mister? We don't get many strangers around here."

"Just walked in from the desert," Cage said, and tried to muster up a halfway friendly smile.

"I can believe that. No offense, hon, but you look like five miles of bad road. Better move into the shade before you keel over from heatstroke."

He stepped under the awning that hung over the post office entrance. "I'll be fine as soon as I find a phone," he said. "Or a garage. Or preferably both."

"Well, you're in luck," she said as she lifted her arms to straighten her ponytail. The action tightened the thin cotton of her shirt across her breasts, which Cage was pretty sure she was well aware of. "Most any business along Main Street will let you use their phone and we happen to have a pretty good mechanic in town. And if you flash those dimples again…" She gave him a wink. "Somebody might even rustle you up a drink. You look like you could use one."

"I wouldn't say no to a cold beer."

"I just bet you wouldn't." She gave him a knowing smile. "Well, then, you just head on up to Lester's garage. You can't miss it. It'll be on your left, just past the beauty shop. Once you're done there, have him point you in the direction of Del Fuego's. Coldest beer in town."

"Thanks."

"You bet."

She hesitated for a moment, as if waiting for another response. When Cage merely nodded, she shrugged. "See you around, stranger." Then she headed into the post office without a backward glance.

Five minutes later, Cage stood in front of a dilapidated building with a dirt parking lot and a faded sign out front with moveable letters that had once spelled GARAGE. Now it read G RAGE.

It had occurred to Cage about two seconds after the blonde disappeared into the post office that she'd been angling for an invitation to join him for a drink. In another time, another place, he might have made the effort to set something up with her, but right now he had more pressing matters on his mind than taking a beautiful woman to bed.

Which just went to show how pathetically desperate he really was.

The smell of rubber and motor oil permeated the air as he walked up to the open bay and rang the bell mounted on the side of the wall.

After a few moments, a young man in greasy coveralls appeared in the doorway. "Help you?"

As Cage briefly explained the situation, the mechanic took off his cap and mopped the back of his neck with the same filthy rag he'd used to wipe his hands.

"Sounds like a busted radiator hose all right," he said when Cage was finished.

Cage glanced at the car inside the garage. "I can probably fix it myself if you're all tied up. All I need is a new hose."

"I won't have anything in stock that'll fit that make and model. You'll have to get it from the parts store."

"Okay. Where's that?"

"Nearest one is in Redford. That's twenty miles east of here. I'm heading over there first thing in the morning for some brake pads. I can pick up a hose for you then if you want me to."

"That won't do me much good," Cage said. "I need to be in El Paso no later than five o'clock today."

Lester shook his head. "Sorry, mister, but you won't be going anywhere with that busted radiator hose."

He was right about that.

Mentally, Cage tallied up the cash he had on hand. "How much will it take to persuade you to make that trip to Redford today instead of in the morning?"

Lester seemed to consider the proposition for a moment, then shook his head. "I'd like to help you out, but I'm right in the middle of a transmission overhaul."

"Fifty dollars," Cage said. "That'll pay your gas and then some for a trip you're going to have to make anyway."

"Like I said, I'd like to help you out and all, but I just don't see how—"

"A hundred bucks." That would take a big bite out of his wallet, but Cage didn't see any other way around it. Besides, he had a company credit card he could always fall back on.

"All right. You got yourself a deal." Lester tossed the rag into a rusted-out barrel and waited patiently while Cage counted out the money.

"Fifty now, fifty when you get back," he said. "That okay with you?"

"Fair enough, I guess." Lester stuffed the money in the back pocket of his coveralls. "Where can I find you when I get back?"

"You know of a place called Del Fuego's?"

"Just down the street a ways. Not much to look at, but the beer's always cold."

"That's what I hear," Cage said.

BUT DEL FUEGO'S WENT well beyond not much to look at.

Hole in the wall was Cage's first impression. The squat building with a flat roof and sagging wooden door reminded him of the places in Saigon his old man used to talk about.

Walk in for a drink, lucky you didn't leave with your damn throat slit.

For all Cage knew, that story was just a load of crap like all the rest of the lies the old man used to spew. He probably hadn't even left stateside during the Vietnam era.

Cage might have wondered if his father had actually been in the service, but he'd seen pictures of him in uniform. A handsome, smiling guy with sparkling white teeth and a full head of hair.

The man in those photographs bore little resemblance to the washed-up drunk who'd deserted his family when Cage was barely thirteen.

After a while, his mother had put away all those old pictures, but Cage had once heard her tell her sister that she still sometimes dreamed about his father, the way he'd been before Vietnam had turned him into a stranger. She still secretly hoped that man would someday come back to her.

His mother's confession had stunned Cage. It was hard for him to reconcile the romantic dreamer pining for her first love with the downtrodden cynic Darleen had become. But then, there were things about his own life that Cage couldn't reconcile.

A fly buzzed around his face as he stepped through the door and stood for a moment glancing around. A bar to his left ran the length of the place, but the five or six patrons were all seated around a table in the back. The light was so dim, Cage could barely make out their features, but he knew he had their attention. He heard a mutter in Spanish, followed by a mocking guffaw.

Ignoring the stares, he slid onto a stool and placed his phone on the bar.

After a moment, the bartender threw a towel over his shoulder and sidled over to Cage. "What can I get for you?"

"*Cerveza,*" Cage said. "Whatever you've got that's cold."

"A man with discerning tastes, I see." The bartender reached for a chilled mug.

"Discerning, no," Cage said. "Parched, yes."

The bartender gave him a curious glance. "Haven't seen you in here before."

"Never been in before, but you come highly recommended." Cage picked up the beer and took a thirsty swallow. "Damn, that's good."

"You sound surprised."

"No, just appreciative."

"Well, it's always nice to be appreciated. I'm Frank Grimes, by the way."

"Cage Nichols."

"Pleased to make your acquaintance, Cage." They shook hands.

"Likewise."

Frank Grimes was a tall, slender man of about fifty with longish gray hair and dancing blue eyes. His faded jeans and madras shirt looked straight out of the sixties, as did the silver peace sign he wore on a black cord around his neck.

He had the look of an artist, Cage decided. The kind that spent his spare time painting coyotes silhouetted against sunsets.

"So, what brings you to our fair town?" Frank folded his arms and leaned against the bar.

"Car trouble," Cage said.

Frank nodded. "A story with which I'm intimately familiar. I was on my way to Juarez when my fuel pump went out just south of town. I had to wait overnight for a part that never came in, and I've been here ever since. That was three years ago."

Cage grimaced. "Well, I hope to have a little better luck than you. I need to be in El Paso by five."

Frank's brows rose. "Five o'clock *today?*"

"Yeah."

"Life or death?"

"More or less."

"That stinks for you, then."

"Tell me about it. I'm still holding out some hope I'll be able to make it on time," Cage said as he took another drink of his beer. "The mechanic at the garage is on his way to Redford now to pick up a part for me."

"You mean Lester?"

"Yeah, that's him."

Frank's eyes twinkled. "How much did you have to pay him?"

"What makes you think I paid him?"

"Because Lester never does anything out of the kindness of his heart. So, how much?"

"Fifty up front and fifty when he returns with the part."

Frank whistled. "That was a big mistake, Cage. You never give Lester anything up front. He gets a little coin in his pocket, you'll be lucky if you see him by the end of the week."

"Damn."

"Damn is right. Might as well have another beer while you wait. I doubt you'll be doing any driving today."

"I don't suppose there's a rental car place in town?" When Frank shook his head, Cage said, "What about a bus?"

"Last westbound Greyhound left two hours ago."

Cage flipped open his cell phone. "What's up with the signal around here?"

"We're in a dead zone," Frank said.

"How the hell can you be in a dead zone? You're out in the middle of nowhere. The signal should be able to travel for miles."

"I've been told it has something to do with electromagnetic currents in the air."

"Personally, I think it's the aliens," a female voice said behind Cage.

He turned to see the blond woman he'd met earlier in front of the post office. For a moment, he flattered himself into thinking she'd come in especially to see him, but then she went around the bar and kissed Frank on the cheek before grabbing an apron from a nearby hook. As she tied it around her slender waist, she gave Cage another one of those knowing smiles.

"See? I told you this place had the coldest beer in town."

"Never mind that we're the *only* place in town," Frank said.

"All the more impressive that we maintain our rigid standards."

Cage hadn't noticed before the way her lips turned up slightly at the corners, or the way her eyes crinkled when she smiled. She really was a very pretty woman.

"So, E.T. or undocumented workers?" he asked, deciding a little flirtation wouldn't do any harm. As long as he was stuck here, he might as well make the wait pleasant.

"Excuse me?"

"You said aliens were responsible for the

cell phone blackout around here," he reminded her.

Frank laughed. "That would be E.T.," he said. "Sadie here drives out to the desert every night with a lawn chair and a six-pack hoping for her very own close encounter."

"Ha-ha, very funny," she said as she took a rag and started wiping down the already spotless bar. "I happen to like watching the desert sky. It's beautiful, and you'd be amazed at some of the things you can see out there."

An argument erupted behind them, and Sadie's smile faded as her gaze shot to the table in the corner. But when Cage started to turn, she put her hand on his arm and said softly, "Nah-uh, hon. Best to mind your own business around here."

"I find it best to do that most everywhere," Cage said.

She nodded. "Smart man."

Someone from the table called out her name. She and Frank exchanged a quick look before she rounded the bar and hurried over to the table.

Cage watched in the mirror as a tall, dark man with a ponytail down his back rose from the table and took Sadie's arm. She flung off his hand and said something in

Spanish, her tone furious. A chortle rose from the group, and she shot a murderous look at the whole table.

"Perros mugrientos," she muttered as she came back over to the bar.

"Everything okay?" Cage asked.

She shrugged.

"Boyfriend trouble?"

"Husband," she said with an apologetic smile.

Cage's gaze dropped to her left hand.

"I don't wear a ring," she said. "It drives Sergio crazy."

"From now on, take the family squabbles outside," Frank said. "I don't want any trouble in here."

"You were asking for trouble the minute you agreed to let them meet here," she warned angrily.

"Why don't you just take the rest of the day off?" Frank said. "I can handle things here."

Sadie glared at him. "No way. I'll tell you the same thing I just told Sergio. I'm not leaving until I'm damn good and ready. Or until you fire me."

"You know I'm not going to fire you," Frank said wearily.

"Then let me stay and do my job. You

won't have any more trouble. Not from Sergio. I'll make sure of that." She turned to Cage with a weak smile. "Sorry about the floor show."

He shrugged. "We've all got problems."

"Another beer?"

"I need to find a phone first."

"There's a pay phone in the back." She waved a hand in the general vicinity. "Need some quarters?"

"I've got a credit card, but thanks."

She picked up his cell phone and slipped it into the pocket of her apron. When he lifted a questioning brow, she grinned. "Insurance, so you don't get the bright idea of skipping out on your bill."

"She's only half joking," Frank said.

"Don't worry, I'll be back. But you do realize that thing is pretty much worthless around here."

Cage knew he was the focus of attention from the men at the table, and he sized them up as best he could from the corner of his eye as he headed toward the back. Three young Hispanics and two middle-aged Caucasians. All thugs, by the looks of them, but Cage wasn't about to involve himself in whatever shady dealings they were plotting. All he wanted to do was get his car running and make tracks for El Paso, the sooner the better.

He located the phone and punched in a series of numbers, including his credit card number. The dark-haired man—Sergio—brushed past him on his way to the restroom. Cage caught a glimpse of a nasty-looking scar that curved around the man's throat before he disappeared through the door.

Cage had seen a scar like that only one other time—on an ex-con who'd had his throat slashed in a prison brawl.

He stared after the man for a moment, then turned back anxiously to the phone when his party answered on the other end.

"It's Cage."

"*¿Qué pasa, tío?*" Andy Sikes drawled jovially. "You already in town?"

"No, that's why I'm calling. I've run into a little trouble on the road."

"What kind of trouble?" Andy asked suspiciously. The two men went back a long way, far enough that Andy was a little too familiar with Cage's track record.

"My car broke down. I'm about a hundred and eighty miles from El Paso in a little Podunk place called San Miguel. Doesn't look good about making that four o'clock meeting."

"Damn it, Cage—"

"I know, I know, you went out on a limb to set it up for me—"

"Jumped through hoops is more like it. It's not just your ass on the line here. If you don't make that meeting, my boss is going to be *muy* ticked off, and that's putting it mildly."

"I hear you. But there's nothing I can do but wait for a part. If I can get on the road within the next hour, I may still be able to make it. It'd help, though, if you'd run a little interference for me."

"Stall, you mean."

"Just for an hour or so."

Andy's exasperated sigh came through loud and clear. "I'll do what I can, but you get your ugly hide to El Paso if you have to sprout wings out your butt and fly here."

"I will. And I owe you one, okay?"

"No, you don't. Let's just call it even. After all, if I hadn't thrown that illegal block sixteen years ago, you might be playing for the Cowboys instead of hustling drill bits for that *pendejo* you call a brother-in-law."

"Water under the bridge. I'll see you in a few hours."

Cage hung up and looked around. He hadn't seen Sergio come out of the bathroom, but he tried the door anyway. It was unlocked and he went in to wash up.

As he stared as his own reflection—the gaunt face, the receding hairline, the tiny grooves that had begun to fan out at the corners of his eyes—he thought again of his father. Maybe he was starting to understand a little of the old man's desperation.

Not much liking what he saw in the mirror, Cage turned on the faucet, and after washing his hands, splashed cold water on his face.

As he was drying off, he noticed that the window was open, and it occurred to him that the reason he hadn't seen Sergio come out of the bathroom was because he'd gone through the window. Evidently, he was giving someone the slip—

A woman's scream brought Cage's head around with a jerk. In two strides he was across the room and flung back the door a split second before another sound registered...the steady *spit-spit-spit* of silenced weapons.

In the space of a heartbeat, Cage took in the bloody massacre as he stood there in the doorway. Two of the men at the table were slumped over in their chairs and a third had fallen to the floor. The fourth had tried to crawl toward the door and now lay twitching in a deepening pool of red.

Cage saw a bloody hand protruding from the end of the bar, and he recognized Sadie's pink nail polish. She was clutching his cell phone. Two crimson splatters on the wall behind the bar marked the spot where she and Frank had been caught by the bullets.

The gunmen were still inside the bar. They were young white guys, unmasked, dressed in jeans and T-shirts. As one of them pumped another round into the man on the floor, the shooter nearest the bar looked up and caught Cage's eye in the mirror. His reflexes seemed almost supernatural as he spun and fired in one fluid movement.

Cage jumped back into the bathroom and slammed the door.

During the hospital stay after his shooting, he'd often wondered what would happen if he found himself again on the wrong end of a loaded weapon. Would he freeze up? Beg for mercy? Roll over and play dead?

Now he had his answer. Instinct and training wouldn't allow for any of those things.

Cage did the only thing he could do. He dove through the window and ran like hell.

Chapter Three

Keeping to the alleys and using the buildings for cover, Cage made his way back around to Main Street.

He had in mind to locate the sheriff's office, constable, or whatever manner of law enforcement was to be found in a place that size. Even a town as tiny as San Miguel would have some kind of peace officer, who in turn would be able to summon the state police or highway patrol to provide backup. Without a weapon, Cage was pretty much useless.

Still, he hadn't given up on the notion of finding a way back inside the bar. He couldn't desert Sadie and Frank without knowing for certain they were dead, and he also didn't like the idea of leaving his cell phone. It would be too easy for the bad guys to trace it back to him. Right now, anonymity was on his side. The gunmen couldn't possibly know who he was.

Cage eased around the corner of a building. One of the shooters stood just outside the bar while the other was still presumably looking for him. Cage ducked back and flattened himself against the wall.

After a moment, he glanced around the corner again. A squad car raced up the street and slid to a halt at the curb. A man in a khaki uniform and aviator glasses got out and propped his arm on the open door. After he and the gunman conversed, the cop strolled leisurely over to the bar and glanced inside.

So much for getting help from the state police, Cage thought grimly.

As he continued to watch, the second gunman came jogging out of a nearby alley. While the three conferred, another vehicle pulled up behind the squad car.

Cage recognized the expensive SUV. It was the same one he'd seen earlier, passing through town.

Two men in dark suits and sunglasses got out. Cage was pretty sure they were cops, too, but a little higher up on the food chain.

One of the gunmen stepped forward and pointed to the bar, then gestured toward the alley from which he'd emerged a few moments earlier, undoubtedly trying to explain how he'd let a witness to the shooting get away from him.

The men in dark suits listened without comment, then the taller of the two reached up and removed his sunglasses. Turning, his eyes traveled slowly over the buildings across the street, as if some instinct drew his gaze straight to Cage.

Cage jerked back, but not before he'd gotten a good look at the man's face. He'd never seen a crueler expression or a colder pair of eyes, and that was saying something considering the lowlifes he'd encountered.

It was only a matter of time before they found out who he was. Only a matter of minutes if they already had his cell phone. Or found his car.

As the five men fanned out, Cage decided it was time to get the hell out of Dodge.

Slipping behind the buildings along Main Street to the garage, he grabbed a couple of water bottles from Lester's cooler and headed out of town the same way he'd come in.

"GRACE! SHERIFF STEELE, I mean. Are you okay?"

"I think so." Grace was sitting on the bottom stair massaging her right ankle when the front door burst open, and Ethan Brennan rushed in. Ethan worked in the county clerk's office and was a friend of Lily's. Platonic friend, she insisted, but it had taken Grace about two seconds in Ethan's company to figure out he had it bad for her sister.

He was just shy of thirty and cute in that intense, techno-geek kind of way. Shoving his dark glasses up his nose, he hurried over to Grace. "What happened?"

"Good question," Grace muttered as she turned and glanced up the stairs. Had someone really pushed her from behind, or had it all happened so fast that she'd only imagined the hand on her back, the face at the top of the stairs?

Luckily, the suitcases that had tumbled down with her had somewhat cushioned her fall. Grace gingerly rotated her ankle. It wasn't broken, thank goodness, but she was already starting to feel the bumps and bruises where she'd been banged around on the stairs.

She looked up into Ethan's anxious face and mustered up a shaky smile. "What are you doing out here anyway?"

He held up a large envelope. "Lily asked me to come by and drop off some papers. When I didn't see her car, I thought she might be down at the barn, so I checked there first. Then I came back up here and I found the front door ajar. I got a little nervous—" His cheeks reddened. "I probably shouldn't have just barged in like that."

"It's okay."

"I didn't know what to think when no one answered my knock—"

"Ethan, it's fine. I'm sure you were worried about Lily."

His blush deepened as his gaze slid away from Grace. He glanced around at all the suitcases strewn about the foyer. "What did happen here?"

"I fell down the stairs."

"You—" His gaze lifted to the staircase behind her and widened. "All the way down? You're lucky you didn't break your neck!"

"No kidding."

"How did you manage to do that?"

"Not break my neck?"

"Fall," he said seriously.

Grace paused. Did she really want to get into her suspicions with Ethan? With anyone, for that matter. Best just to keep her mouth shut until she had a chance to look around. "I'm not sure how it happened. Maybe I hooked my heel on the rug or something. I had my arms full and couldn't see where I was going."

His gaze went back to the suitcases. "So…you're leaving?"

"I'm just moving into town. Maybe you could give me a hand with all this stuff."

"Be glad to. Just let me put this somewhere first." He placed the envelope on a table near the stairs, then turned back to Grace. "It's for Lily," he said.

"So you said."

He gave her a sheepish grin that Grace found adorable. How could Lily not just eat him up with a spoon?

"Are you sure you're okay?" He offered her a hand as she got to her feet.

"Just a few bruises. See?" She put weight on her ankle. "No permanent harm done."

"Thank goodness. First Sheriff Dickerson and now you. People might start to think there's a curse on this town."

"Well, we wouldn't want that, would we?" Grace's attention was caught by a passing shadow out one of the side windows. A few minutes later, she heard footsteps on the porch, and then Lily appeared in the doorway.

Her dark hair, which she wore in a braid down her back, was slightly askew and she appeared out of breath. She had on jeans and a cotton shirt, which had become the unofficial uniform of the deputies in Criminal Investigations except on days when they had to appear in court.

The lax dress code had bothered Grace at first, but after a few days of coping with the heat and the rugged West Texas terrain, she'd eased up on her expectations.

Since Grace hadn't heard a vehicle drive up, she had to assume that Lily had been there all along. While Grace had been talking with Ethan, her sister would have had plenty of time to go down the rear staircase and out the back door, then make her way around to the front of the house.

Grace tried to check the direction of her thoughts. Did she really think her own sister had pushed her down the stairs?

"What's going on?" Lily asked as she stepped through the door.

"Your sister just fell down the stairs," Ethan blurted.

"Really? All the way down?" Her eyes collided with Grace's. Lily didn't seem overly concerned, or even surprised, to hear about the incident. In fact, Grace's stomach churned at the passive expression on her sister's face.

"I told her she's lucky she didn't break her neck," Ethan said.

"Well, you always did have all the luck in the family." Lily's cool gaze swept back to Grace. "What was it Mama used to say? The more things change, the more they stay the same?"

"But—" Ethan shifted uncomfortably.

"What?" Lily snapped.

"You don't—"

She put a hand on her hip. "I don't *what?*"

"Grace could have been seriously hurt," Ethan said.

"But she wasn't. Were you, Grace?"

"I'm fine."

"Of course you are. No one knows better than you how to take care of Number One. Am I right?"

"If you say so." Grace wasn't about to rise to Lily's bait. She had no intention of airing their dirty laundry in front of Ethan Brennan or anyone else. It was bad enough that Lily could barely remain civil at work.

Her sister spotted the envelope Ethan had put on the table and pounced on it. "Is that for me?"

"It's all in there," Ethan said. "Everything you requested—"

"Thanks." She glanced inside the envelope,

then placed it back on the table. As she turned, she made a point of toeing one of Grace's suitcases out of her way. "So you're splitting, huh?"

"That's what you want, isn't it?"

Lily's gaze lifted, and the coldness in those gray depths sent a shiver down Grace's spine. "You have no idea what I want. You never did."

Suddenly, an image of that face at the top of the stairs came back to Grace. She couldn't say with any certainty that it had been Lily up there peering down at her, and she wanted desperately to believe that it had not been. But dread tightened like a fist around Grace's heart. What if it *had* been Lily?

What if her own sister…had just tried to kill her?

THE DESERT WAS NOT an ideal place to hide, Cage soon discovered as he made his way back to his car.

Putting the manual transmission in neutral, he pushed the vehicle as far out into the barren landscape as he could manage. He hated like hell to abandon it. That car was about the only thing he owned free and clear these days. But in his current fix, there wasn't much else he could do.

Getting out his map, he decided the best way to evade his hunters was to stay off all roads that led into or out of San Miguel. There was another highway about ten or fifteen miles due west across the desert where he might be able to find a phone or hitch a ride.

He glanced up at the blazing sun. He'd be crossing in the heat of the day, but he had two water bottles and he damn sure had the will to live.

Down on his luck was a helluva lot better than dead, Cage decided as he buried the license plates from his car and the contents of his glove box in the sand.

Chapter Four

Ethan helped Grace carry her bags to the truck while Lily watched from the front porch. When Grace went back in to get the last of her things, Lily followed her inside.

She picked up the envelope and tapped it against her palm. "You may as well know," she said. "I'm putting the ranch on the market."

Grace looked up in surprise. "When did you decide to do that?"

"I've been thinking about it for a long time. I've already talked to Rachel. She says to do whatever I want. She'll sign the papers."

Grace tried to shrug off the stab of betrayal she felt over Rachel's silence. She wasn't surprised to be the last person Lily would talk to about this, but why hadn't Rachel called her? "When were the two of you going to tell me about it?"

Lily's eyes glinted with a touch of defiance. "I'm telling you now."

"Do you have a buyer?"

"I've had some interest. No firm offers yet."

"Where will you go?"

Lily shrugged. "I don't know. Find a place in town, I guess. Or maybe it's time that I move on altogether."

"Leave Jericho Pass, you mean?"

She tossed her braid over her shoulder. "Why not? You and Rachel couldn't wait to get out of this place. Now that Grandma Stella's dead, there's nothing keeping me here, either." *Especially now that you're back,* her eyes seemed to taunt.

A sound from the front porch brought both women around in surprise. Grace had forgotten all about Ethan, but there he stood watching them.

He cleared his throat. "Sorry. I didn't mean to eavesdrop. I just came back to see if I could give you a hand with anything else."

Grace supposed the offer had been posed to her, but Ethan couldn't take his eyes off Lily. He looked crestfallen, and Grace thought she knew why. Given his position at the county clerk's office, he probably knew or at least suspected that Lily had plans to sell the ranch, but Grace was almost certain that until that very moment, he'd never contemplated the possibility of her sister actually leaving town.

When he realized that Grace was studying him, he quickly glanced away.

Lily, of course, noticed none of this. Where Ethan Brennan was concerned, she seemed completely oblivious.

"I think that's the last of it," Grace told him. "Thanks for the help."

"Any time." His gaze crept back to her sister. "See you around, Lily."

She seemed to catch herself then and said, "Yeah, thanks for everything, Ethan."

"Glad to help out." He hesitated, obviously hoping for another bone, then turned with a defeated little shrug and left.

Grace waited until she heard the screen door close before she faced Lily. "You could have left Jericho Pass anytime you wanted. Why now? Is it because I'm back?"

Anger flared in Lily's eyes. "Newsflash, Grace. Not everything is about you. If I decide to leave town, it'll be because it's what *I* want."

Grace stared at her in exasperation. "Why the attitude, Lily? What did I ever do to you?"

Her sister folded her arms. "Like you don't know."

"It can't be just about the job," Grace said helplessly. "You've been like this for years. Why don't you just tell me so we can try to work it out? We're sisters. It shouldn't be like this between us."

Lily smiled. "Well, see, that's the beauty of it, Grace. You don't get to control how I feel about you."

She turned and bounded up the stairs, then paused on the landing to stare back down at Grace. "Ethan was right, you know. You're lucky you didn't break your neck."

THE SUN WAS ALREADY going down when Cage finally spotted the highway up ahead. He'd been walking due west since he set out, and early on, the light had been blinding. Now, as the sun sank below the horizon, the sky turned blood red, then deepened to a gilded violet.

As he gazed upward, Cage thought of Sadie and the way Frank had teased her about hoping for a close encounter. *You'd be amazed at what you can see out there,* she'd said. Cage couldn't help wondering now if she'd witnessed more than just a starry sky on her nightly excursions to the desert. Was there a reason she'd been shot, other than being at the wrong place at the wrong time?

Cage had a bad feeling the massacre at Del Fuego's was only the tip of the iceberg. Corruption and drug trafficking were nothing new along the border, but he didn't think what he'd stumbled into was some penny-ante deal gone south.

In spite of their youth, the shooters were highly trained professionals. And the men in suits looked to be upper crust law enforcement. State level, at least. Maybe even FBI or DEA, which left Cage with few options. If he called the state police, they'd likely haul his ass in for questioning, and until he managed to convince someone to believe him, he'd be a sitting duck in custody. Eventually, the truth might come out, but with cops involved, he could be dead by then.

So, at the moment, he had only one clear course of action. Put as much distance as he could between himself and San Miguel.

About a hundred yards up the road, Cage spotted a car pulled to the shoulder. He hesitated, wondering if he should approach or head off in the opposite direction.

Hunkering down at the edge of the desert,

he waited several minutes, but he didn't see any movement. He might have thought the car had stalled and the driver had taken off on foot like he'd had to do earlier, but the top was down and he could hear the radio.

The twang of an electric guitar seemed a good enough omen to Cage, and he decided to move in a little closer, see if he could detect any sign of life.

The car was an old black Cadillac Eldorado, beautifully restored, with high tailfins and a low slung profile that looked about a mile long. Cage took a moment to appreciate the classic lines before he inched in, keeping an eye on the road behind him and the desert on either side of him.

Easing up to the driver's side, he glanced in. The key was in the ignition. Whoever the car belonged to couldn't have gone far—

"Hold it right there, mister."

Cage straightened. A man stood on the other side of the car pointing a gun at him.

"Back away from the vehicle," the man said gruffly. "Easy does it, slick."

Cage lifted his hands and took a step back from the car.

The man kept a bead drawn on Cage as he slowly rounded the rear of the Caddy.

"You weren't thinking about trying to steal my car, were you, boy?"

"No, sir," Cage said. "I was hoping I might hitch a ride."

"That a fact."

They took a moment to size each other up in the gloom.

Then the driver nodded toward the desert. "What the hell you doing way off out here in the middle of nowhere on foot?"

"My car broke down a ways back," Cage said. "Cell phone wouldn't work so I had no choice but to hoof it."

"I just came from thata way myself," the man said. "I didn't see no broken-down car. Didn't see much of nuthin' but a prairie-dog town."

"I pushed the car off the road so it wouldn't get stripped before I could make it back with a part."

"That's city-boy thinking. You ain't from around here, are you?"

"Just passing through," Cage said. "Never been out west before. Thought I'd like to see it before I die."

"You don't expect that to be imminent, do you?"

"Hope not."

The man seemed to consider Cage's explanation. He looked to be in his early to mid-forties, but he had the kind of round, boyish face that made age hard to determine, especially in the dusky light.

He was average height, with broad shoulders and a wide chest that seemed to strain the pearl snaps of his western shirt, and a gut that was just starting to protrude over his silver belt buckle.

As he eyed Cage suspiciously, he shifted the gun to his left hand and used his right wrist to wipe away what Cage thought at first was sweat from his brow. Then he saw that it was blood.

"Hey, mister, you okay?"

"I've been better." When he edged around the car to open the front door, Cage got a better look at him. He was flushed and his breathing sounded strained. "Just need to sit down for a minute," he said and waved his gun toward Cage. "Better not get any bright ideas, though. I can pick a fly off that cactus over yonder even with a pea shooter like this."

"Gotcha." Cage backed up another step. "That's a pretty nasty-looking cut. You may need some stitches in that thing."

"I'll get it cleaned up soon as I hit the next town."

"How far is that?"

"Thirty, forty miles." His breathing was becoming more labored by the minute. Cage thought he looked on the verge of passing out.

"What happened to you, anyway?"

"Been on the road for hours. Started feeling poorly so I pulled over and got out to walk around for a spell." He took another swipe at the blood trickling down his face. "Damned if I didn't pass clean out. Never done that before in my life. Must have hit my head on the bumper when I went down. Didn't feel a damn thing."

"Look, it's none of my business," Cage said. "But you really need to get to a hospital. You don't look so hot."

"Don't feel so hot. But I can still put a lead cap in your ass, you try anything."

"Tell you what," Cage said. "I need a ride and you need a driver. What do you say we help each other out?"

"Do I look like the kind of ignoramus that goes around picking up strangers? Why, hellfire, boy, for all I know, you could be one of them serial killers I read so much about. I pass out again, you're apt to slit my throat and steal my car."

"Mister, if I wanted to steal your car, I'd already be ten miles down the road by now."

He drew another bead. "You sure about that, son?"

Cage grinned. "Pretty sure, yeah."

"Big talker," the man said, and then he laughed. "But damned if I don't believe you."

"WHAT'S YOUR NAME, SON?" the stranger asked over the roar of the wind as the convertible glided like a sailboat down the highway.

Cage hesitated as he pretended to fiddle with the rearview mirror. "Frank. Frank Grimes."

"Pleased to meet you, Frank. I'm Dale Walsh."

"Where you headed, Dale?"

"Up the road a ways."

"Where you coming from?"

"Galveston."

Cage shot him a glance. "You're a long way from home. What brings you out west?"

"On my way to see a man about a job."

"Oh, yeah?"

"Yeah. I'm headed to a place called Jericho Pass. Ever hear of it?" He laid his head back against the red leather seat and closed his eyes.

"Can't say as I have." Cage's gaze dropped to the gun that rested on the top of Dale Walsh's thigh. "What do you do?"

"I guess you could say I'm a people person."

"People person?" Cage said. "You mean like, sales or something?"

"Or something. Business ain't been so great lately. Damn recession's killing me."

"I hear that," Cage muttered. "So, what do you sell?"

When Dale didn't respond, he glanced over at him. "Hey, Dale? You okay over there?"

Dale's head lolled back against the seat. "I don't feel so good."

"So you said. You need me to pull over?"

"No, just keep driving, boy. I think you better get me to a doctor real quick. Something's not right."

"Hang in there," Cage said. "And try to stay awake, okay? That head injury worries me."

"I just need to rest my eyes a spell."

"Here. How about I turn back on some music? Maybe you could try singing along or something."

He turned up the volume, but Dale was already looking pretty out of it and Cage was starting to worry that he might be more seriously hurt than either of them had first thought. Head injuries could be deceptive. Cage had seen a guy walk away from a car crash once, perfectly lucid with only a few scratches and bruises, only to die a few hours later from brain swelling.

Hitching a ride with a guy on death's door was not exactly the way he'd planned to make his getaway, but there was nothing he could do now but get the poor bastard to a doctor.

As they neared the next town, Cage stopped at the first gas station they came to and asked about a hospital. By the time he drove up to the E.R. entrance, Dale was unconscious. When Cage couldn't rouse him, he flagged down a couple of orderlies to help him.

They loaded Dale onto a stretcher and whisked him into the hospital. The woman behind the desk gave Cage some paperwork to fill out.

"But I don't even know the guy," Cage said as he looked down at the form.

"Just do the best you can," she said wearily. "When you're finished, bring it back up here to me."

Cage sat down in the noisy emergency room and looked over the questionnaire. A news broadcast on the television caught his attention, and when he looked up, he saw a map on the screen with San Miguel circled in red.

He laid aside the clipboard and went over to the television so that he could hear over the E.R. chatter.

The bodies of six gunshot victims including one female had been found in a bar in the small border town of San Miguel in Presidio County. A man who was seen entering the establishment was wanted for questioning in the shooting, which authorities believed was drug related. The suspect was described as being a white male, midthirties, six feet tall, lean, and walked with a noticeable limp.

Cage stared at the news anchor in shock. She'd just described him. *He* was the suspect.

And it was a damn clever ploy, too. By going public with his description, the bad guys would have every local lawman and highway patrol officer in the area on the alert for a man fitting his description. Cage had just become the target of every hotshot cop in West Texas looking to make a name for himself.

"Sir?"

Cage spun, startled. The man who had come up behind him was a doctor, not a cop, thank goodness.

He gave Cage a curious look. "Are you the man who brought in the heart-attack victim?"

Cage shook his head. "I brought in a guy with a gash in his head."

"Came in about twenty minutes ago, unconscious, laceration above his right eyebrow?"

"Yeah, that's him."

"I'm sorry to tell you he didn't make it."

"Didn't make it," Cage repeated. "What happened?"

"It had nothing to do with the head injury. He suffered a massive coronary. We did everything we could, but we couldn't revive him."

A heart attack? No wonder the poor guy hadn't looked so good.

The doctor was waiting for some kind of response. "That's a real shame," Cage said. It was lame, but he didn't know what else to say at the moment. It was all he could do to keep his gaze from straying back to the television. "He seemed like a nice guy."

"I take it you're not the next of kin?"

"No, I'm afraid not. I don't know anything about him. We just met out on the road a little while ago."

"There was no identification among his personal effects. Do you at least know his name?"

"His name…" Cage trailed off. A uniformed police officer had just come into the E.R. and was talking to the woman behind the desk.

Cage's heart started to beat a quick, painful staccato. The last thing he needed right now was to attract the attention of the authorities.

"Sir? Are you okay?"

He glanced back at the doctor. "Yeah, I just…give me a minute, will you? This has all been kind of a shock. I think I need to go splash some cold water on my face or something."

"The restrooms are right over there." The doctor nodded toward the hallway.

"Thanks."

Cage went into the bathroom, waited a minute, then glanced out. The cop and the receptionist were still conversing at the desk. Whether their discussion had anything to do with him or Dale Walsh, Cage had no idea. What he did know, though, was that he had to somehow get the hell out of there without being noticed.

He waited until they were looking the other way, and then he slipped down the hallway, found another exit, and a few minutes later, sped out of town in Dale Walsh's old black Cadillac.

As soon as he was far enough from town to feel confident he wasn't being pursued, Cage pulled off on a side road and sat with the engine idling while he went through the contents of the glove box. He found nothing inside that indicated how he could get in touch with Dale Walsh's next of kin. He stuffed the odds and ends back inside the compartment along with Dale's .38. Then he got out and walked back to the trunk.

There was a small suitcase inside, along with a silver briefcase. Thumbing open the latches of the metal case, Cage raised the lid and whistled.

Inside he found a pair of custom-made AMT Hardballers fitted with silencers, a stack of cash and a large envelope containing a photograph of a woman and a typewritten note which read: *5 grand now, the other 5 when the bitch is dead.*

People person my ass, Cage thought.

Chapter Five

The more miles Cage put between himself and the dead hit man, the more he thought about the woman in the photograph. Her image had started to haunt him.

He kept telling himself it was not his concern. He had his own problems to deal with. Best thing to do was stick to his latest plan, which was to get to El Paso as quickly as he could.

Once there, he'd catch a flight back to Dallas where he still had contacts in law enforcement that he trusted, and even a few friends in high places that might be able to help him get out of this mess in one piece.

Besides, he didn't know the name of Dale Walsh's target, so how was he supposed to warn her?

He didn't know her name, but he had a pretty good idea where she lived. Walsh had said he was on his way to Jericho Pass to see a man about a job.

Cage drummed his fingers impatiently on the steering wheel. So what should he do?

Just get to El Paso and figure out the rest when you arrive. Only thing you can do. This isn't your problem.

Besides, Walsh could have been lying about Jericho Pass. Would a hit man really be so brazen about his destination?

Maybe, if he hadn't planned on Cage outliving him.

Earlier, Cage had put the Caddy's top up because it made him feel less exposed. Now he turned on the radio, hoping some music would take his mind off that photograph.

But it was hard to get a woman like that out of his head. Whoever she was, she was a damn fine-looking woman. Not that appearances mattered, but Cage couldn't help admiring all that black glossy hair, those shiny full lips. And her eyes. Man, he'd always been a sucker for dark, soulful eyes.

And someone wanted her dead. Ten-thousand-dollars-worth of dead.

When Cage finally saw the exit for Jericho Pass, he wondered if it was an omen, good or bad, that the song playing on the radio was ELO's "Showdown."

BY THE TIME CAGE LOCATED the sheriff's office, he'd formulated a new plan. He'd leave the briefcase and everything inside— the guns, money and photograph—in a prominent spot at the station, along with a note that he'd already composed in his head.

There's a photograph of a woman inside this briefcase. Someone hired a hit man to kill her. He's dead, but they might send someone else. Better find her and warn her ASAP.

Cage was still a cop at heart, so leaving a note and then slipping away like a thief in the night went against his grain.

But he didn't know how else to handle the situation. He couldn't afford to show his face inside a police station, let alone be interrogated by whoever happened to be on duty. He knew how that would work. He'd face a barrage of questions he mostly couldn't answer and then they'd throw him in a holding cell until they could check out his story.

And once they ran his prints and started making official inquiries…*good night, Irene.* The dirtbags from San Miguel would know exactly where to find him.

So, the warning had to be issued anonymously. There was just no way around it that he could see.

Besides, he didn't know anything more than what he'd tell them in the note. His message, along with the guns, money and the note that spelled out the transaction should be enough to convince the authorities that the woman in the photograph was in imminent danger.

After he scribbled the warning on the back of a receipt he'd dug out of the glove box, Cage got out of the car, opened the trunk and grabbed the briefcase.

The parking lot in front of the one-story brick station was nearly empty. This time of night, he'd counted on a scaled-down force. He'd be able to leave the case and note near the entrance, then hightail it out of town—

"Hey, you!"

At the sound of the male voice behind him, Cage hesitated but didn't turn.

"Hey, I said wait up!"

Cage glanced over his shoulder. A uniformed deputy came hurrying across the well-lit parking lot toward him.

Cage's first instinct was to climb back in the car and try to take off before the guy caught up with him. But the last thing he needed was a nasty confrontation, especially one in which the outcome might not be in his favor.

The deputy had at least a couple of inches and twenty pounds on him, the kind of fellow who would have looked downright menacing even without the huge firearm strapped to his thigh. Cage was exhausted and his knee hurt like a son of a bitch. But even on a good day, he wasn't so sure he'd able to take this guy in a fair fight.

"Are you talking to me?" he asked in the most non-threatening tone he could muster.

"Yeah, I'm talking to you."

But the deputy grinned when he said it and not in a puffed-up, arrogant, *I'll show this out-of-town clown who's boss* kind of way, either. He seemed genuinely pleased to see Cage.

Which was…strange.

When the deputy drew closer, he said, "Dale Walsh, right? I would have known you anywhere!"

Cage was completely taken aback. Before he could say anything, the deputy thrust out his hand. "Sam Dickerson. It's a pleasure to finally meet you. Charlie Dickerson's my uncle. Man, he's been singing your praises ever since y'all met at that San Antonio conference a while back."

"Good to hear," Cage muttered as he shook the man's hand.

"I guess you're wondering how I recognized you," Deputy Dickerson said, still with that idiotic grin on his face.

"Thought did cross my mind."

"This baby right here, is how." The beaming deputy nodded toward the Cadillac. "Uncle C said you had the best-looking Eldorado Biarritz he ever did see, and, man, oh man, he wasn't lying. This thing is a work of art." He ran his hand lovingly over the mile-high tailfin. "Looks just like a damn rocket. Less than fifteen hundred of these beauties were built in 1959. But I'm guessing you already knew that."

"Yeah, she's something, all right," Cage said.

The deputy chuckled. "That's an understatement if I ever heard one. You'll have to pardon my drool, but I'm a classic car buff from way back. Me and Uncle C both. He's got a '57 Corvette he's been working on for years. Me, I'm more of a Thunderbird man."

Cage thought of the car he'd had to abandon in the desert. Not a classic by any means, but he was still sorry to let it go. It was highly doubtful the vehicle would still be there if and when he ever ventured back that way.

Sam Dickerson rubbed his hands together. "I'd dearly love to take a gander at that 345 under the hood, but I imagine the sheriff's expecting you inside, right?"

Cage murmured something unintelligible as he glanced toward the front of the station. His encounter with Deputy Dickerson was playing hell with his plan.

"I guess you heard about Uncle C." Dickerson started walking toward the station and Cage didn't know what else to do but follow. "Throat cancer. I guess that's what happens when you chew tobacco for as long as he did. I can't ever remember seeing him without a chaw."

"Well, here's hoping he makes a speedy recovery," Cage said. Even though his knee was on fire, he gritted his teeth and made sure he didn't limp.

"Oh, he'll pull through all right. He's a tough old bird. But he's got a long row to hoe, that's for damn sure." The deputy opened the glass door to the station. "Maybe I should warn you about something. The acting sheriff is female," he said. "I hope you're not bothered by that sort of thing."

"Nope, not a problem." Cage couldn't care

less about the sex of the new sheriff. His only concern at the moment was how best to disentangle himself from this latest complication. "Male chauvinism is so last century."

The deputy laughed good-naturedly at the lame quip. "We may be a little behind the times out here, but nobody can deny this gal has some serious chops. She used to work for the TBI. That's basically the state version of the FBI."

"I'm familiar with the TBI," Cage said. "Impressive credentials."

He had only a brief impression of a large room divided into cubicles and filled with desks before Deputy Dickerson ushered him over to a glass-fronted office to the right. Cage didn't see anyone inside, but the deputy knocked anyway, then opened the door.

"Sheriff Steele? Dale Walsh just got here. Detective Walsh, I should say."

Detective Walsh?

Cage was thrown for another loop. Had Dale Walsh been both a lawman and a hit man?

Well, that just figured, didn't it?

Cage mentally berated himself for his stupidity. Had he really expected just to breeze in here, dump the briefcase and its problems in someone else's lap, then blow town before anyone caught on to him? That would have been too easy. And it would have taken no small element of luck.

Of course, Dale Walsh was both hit man and cop. *Of course,* Deputy Fife over there had had to drive up at precisely the same moment that Cage had picked to dump the case. *Of course,* the guy's uncle, the sheriff, had told him all about Walsh's Caddy. And *of course,* OF COURSE, Dale Walsh was expected here in Jericho Pass, apparently on some kind of official business.

Which, no doubt, would have provided excellent cover while he located his target and carried out the hit. But what it did for Cage was make it near impossible for him to walk out of this place without coming clean. And the moment he did that, he was likely a dead man.

This was all starting to seem like a bad joke, he decided. The whole bizarre setup reeked of divine retribution. He'd been no angel in the past, but this? *Come on.*

The deputy moved back from the door so that Cage could enter the office. He stepped inside, then froze as the chair behind the desk rotated and a woman got up to greet him.

He took one look at the glossy hair and

shiny lips, those dark, soulful eyes, and his heart gave a strange little flip.

She was the woman whose photograph was in the metal briefcase he carried at his side, along with the guns, the cash and a note which read: *5 grand now, and the other 5 when the bitch is dead.*

Cage shot a glance skyward.

You gotta be kiddin' me.

DALE WALSH WASN'T EXACTLY what Grace had been expecting. From Charlie Dickerson's description, she'd thought he'd be a little older. Early forties, at least. This man looked only a year or two older than she.

Not that it mattered. And not that she had to speculate. If everything worked out, Grace would learn all she needed to know about Dale Walsh from the paperwork he'd be required to fill out and from the background check she'd order on him.

But from Charlie's notes alone, she'd already gleaned that Walsh had an impressive record with the Galveston Police Department. Of course, that didn't mean he'd have the right stuff for what he'd be dealing with out here. The counties and communities along the border had their own special set of problems.

The official story on Walsh would come later, but for now, Grace wanted to rely on her instincts. She'd always been a big believer in first impressions, so she tried to size him up in the split second it took for her to round the desk and offer her hand.

He was tall and a little on the lean side, though she suspected there might be some serious muscles hidden by the long sleeves of his shirt. He looked strong and capable, and she appreciated the way he gripped her hand as he looked her straight in the eyes.

"I'm Grace Steele," she said. "We were expecting you a little earlier, Detective Walsh."

"Pleasure to meet you, Sheriff. I apologize for being so late. And for my appearance." He brushed off his dusty pants. "I ran into a little trouble out on the road. Had some cell phone problems, too, so I couldn't call ahead and let you know when to expect me. I hope you didn't wait around on my account."

"I'm almost always here this late, so no harm done." She waved toward the chair across from her desk. "Have a seat."

Deputy Dickerson said from the doorway, "Catch you later, Dale."

"Yeah, thanks," he said with a brief wave. Grace noticed that Walsh waited until she'd taken a seat behind the desk before he sat. Carefully, he placed his briefcase on the floor beside his chair.

"You heard about Charlie Dickerson, I suppose?"

He nodded. "Sam and I were just talking about that. It's a real shame. Charlie's a good guy."

"He sure thinks highly of you."

"Well…that's always nice to hear."

Now that she'd had time to study him, Grace realized he was a little older than she'd first thought. Probably not yet forty, but getting close to it for sure. His brown hair looked to be receding at a pretty good clip, and the lines in his face had deepened to grooves at the corners of his eyes.

Despite his age, he had a boyish charm about him, and his old-world courtliness intrigued Grace. But it was his eyes that held her attention now. They were the most vivid blue she'd ever encountered, and that piercing color gave the directness of his gaze a pretty powerful punch.

Grace's stomach fluttered as they regarded one another across the expanse of her desk, and she thought, *Oh, damn. Not now. Not with him.*

Her first inclination was to nip that little

ripple of sexual tension in the bud, even if it meant she had to cut the meeting short and send Dale Walsh packing. The last thing she needed or wanted was any kind of awkwardness between her and one of her subordinates.

But dismissing Dale Walsh out of hand after he'd come all this way at her predecessor's request was totally unprofessional. The department was shorthanded and from everything Charlie had told her, Walsh was a good candidate. If she found him attractive, well…that was her problem, not his. Why deprive the county of a good deputy and Dale Walsh of a steady paycheck just because that nasty business in Austin had left her feeling stupid and gun-shy?

What she really needed to do was get a grip, Grace told herself.

She cleared her throat and broke the gaze. "Charlie tells me he's been after you to come in for an interview for quite some time now. Mind telling me why you finally decided to take him up on the offer?"

For the first time since he'd entered her office, Dale Walsh looked unsure of himself. Then he shrugged. "It's no big mystery, really. Sometimes a man just needs a new challenge. New scenery. That's all there is to it."

Grace could appreciate the need for new scenery. After her humiliation before the review board, she hadn't been able to get out of Austin fast enough. But there had been nothing simple about her decision to come back to Jericho Pass, and she wondered if Dale Walsh might have an ulterior motive as well.

"One word of caution," she said. "If you think a rural police department like ours is a place where you can coast, think again. We're seeing a high level of violence down here these days. West Texas is no place for the faint of heart."

"I'm not looking to coast. That's the last thing I want." Walsh leaned in a bit, his expression earnest. "I'm a cop. It's what I do and it's who I am. If I wanted to coast, I'd go off and work for my brother-in-law or something." He smiled, and the commas at the corners of his mouth deepened.

Grace found herself smiling back at him, and she hadn't felt like doing that in a long, long time. Dale Walsh's manner was open and engaging, and she couldn't help responding to him. "I've found that working with family is not for the faint of heart, either," she said.

"I hear that."

She cleared her throat again. "I don't know

how familiar you are with the situation down here, but if you're really looking for a new challenge, you've come to the right place. We've got ranches right across the border that are being used as paramilitary camps by the drug cartels. Their recruits are being trained in the use of all manner of weaponry, including AK-47s, AR-15s, grenade launchers, you name it."

"Sounds like they're planning for a war," he said.

"They're already at war," Grace replied. "Once the cartels started hiring army deserters and ex-members of the Guatemalan Special Forces to militarize their operations, they turned the occasional turf battle into an all-out Armageddon. We've got assassins and narco-terrorists operating on both sides of the border, and so far we've not seen much concern from Washington or the news media. We've been doing what we can on our own, but with limited resources and manpower, it's like taking a pellet gun to a bazooka fight. I'm not trying to scare you off," she added. "I'm just trying to give you a realistic rundown of the situation."

"I appreciate that," Walsh said. "Sounds like you've got a real mess on your hands."

"To put it mildly." Grace studied him for a moment. "I'll be honest. If everything that Charlie told me about your record is true, we'd be lucky to get you. We can always use someone around here with your kind of experience. The pay's lousy and the hours are even worse, so I don't see how you can possibly turn us down," she said with a half smile. "But before either of us makes a final decision, I think you should take some time to think it over. I understand you'll be here for a few days, so why don't we meet back here tomorrow morning and I'll show you around the station, introduce you to some of the staff. I also think it would be a good idea for you to do a bit of exploring. See what a town like this has to offer a guy like you."

He nodded. "Sounds like a plan."

As soon as Grace rose, he stood, too.

"I assume you already have a place to stay while you're here?" she asked.

"Uh, yeah, that's not a problem."

"Then I guess there's only one other thing we need to talk about before we call it a night." She came around the desk and propped a hip against the edge. "When you were first contacted about this position, you had every reason to believe you'd be working for Charlie Dickerson. His return is up in the air at the moment, and for the next several months at least, I'll be in charge of this department. Do you have a problem answering to a female superior?"

Again, he looked her right in the eyes and said without hesitation, "No, ma'am. That's not a problem for me."

Grace appreciated the conviction she heard in his voice. She thrust out her hand and they shook again. "Thanks for making that long trip. I'm glad you didn't cancel once you heard about Charlie."

"Yeah, me, too."

"I'll see you in the morning—let's say, nine o'clock. Is that good for you?"

"Nine o'clock sharp," he agreed, and turned to leave.

"Detective Walsh?"

He hesitated a fraction of a second at the door before he turned. "Yeah?"

She nodded toward the chair he'd just vacated. "You forgot your briefcase."

Something flickered in his eyes before his gaze dropped to the floor. "So I did." He went over and picked up the case, then paused again at the door. "Well, good night."

"Good night."

Grace stood in the doorway and watched him stride across the station. There was much to like about the man, she decided. Even aside from Charlie's glowing recommendation, Dale Walsh had the kind of quiet confidence and innate strength that Grace had always preferred over the in-your-face bravado of some of her male compatriots. He hadn't wavered once in the face of the border crisis she'd described, nor had he so much as blinked when she asked if he had a problem working for a woman.

All that was a definite plus. During her time at the TBI, Grace had seen her share of pandering, condescension and resentment, all solely because of her gender. So, it was refreshing to meet a man who had a healthy sense of himself and was not threatened by a female associate, let alone a superior.

And he seemed to be just a genuinely likable guy.

Of course, her initial assessment of him could always change. She'd been fooled before, unfortunately.

Closing her office door, Grace moved over to the window that looked out on the parking lot. Walsh had been heading toward his car, but he stopped suddenly, glanced over his shoulder, then slowly turned back to the station.

Grace wondered if he might have forgotten something else, but he made no move toward the building. Instead, he stood there for several seconds as if in deep contemplation—or conflict.

Then he seemed to shrug off whatever had held him immobile, and continued on his way across the parking lot.

But as Grace watched him climb into his car and drive off, she couldn't help wondering about those odd little moments of hesitation.

Was Dale Walsh really as open and direct as he'd led her to believe?

Chapter Six

When Cage left the station, he still wasn't sure what he aimed to do about the briefcase. Now that he'd met the target in person, he was having a harder time just walking away.

But he knew he was in no condition to reasonably assess the situation. He was tired, hungry and in pain. What he needed was a shower, some food and a safe place to hole up where he could do some serious thinking and planning.

Stopping by a discount store, he bought a change of clothing, underwear, socks and the essential toiletries he would need to make himself feel human again. He asked the clerk who checked him out for a motel recommendation, and a little while later—after a quick bite at a drive-thru—he found himself at a rooms-for-rent place called Miss Nelda's, which was run, appropriately enough, by a woman named Nelda Van Horn and her sister, Georgina.

The gingerbread-trimmed house was a rambling two-story with a wraparound front porch and a long balcony on the second floor where guests could enjoy panoramic views of the mountains and the spectacular West Texas sunsets.

The sisters looked to be in their seventies, one still a determined blonde, the other an improbable redhead, and neither the least bit shy about giving Cage a long scrutiny that was anything but subtle. They watched him sign the registry, then took a deposit in cash without blinking an eye. Next, they pointed him up the stairs to his room on the second floor.

The first order of business—once Cage had secured both the hallway and balcony doors—was to hide the briefcase behind an old steam radiator. Then he called his sister in Dallas and Andy in El Paso with the excuse that he'd broken down on the road and was spending the night in a town several miles to the east of Jericho Pass so they wouldn't call the police when he didn't turn up. Finally, he stripped off his dusty clothes and climbed into the shower.

After scrubbing the grime of the desert out

of his hair and off his skin, Cage braced himself with his hands against the tile wall and leaned into the water, letting it sluice over his head and down his body until the temperature started to cool. Then he climbed out, dried off and sprawled on the bed, folding his hands behind his head as he stared up at the ceiling.

Grace Steele's suggestion that he stick around town for a few days, however impractical or ill-advised, was starting to have some appeal. If Dale Walsh had been, in fact, both a cop and a hired gun, Cage was now in a unique position to find the sheriff's would-be killer. In all likelihood, the conspirator would contact him the moment he—or she— learned that Walsh had hit town.

On the other hand, the man Cage had met out on the highway might well have been an impostor. In which case, the real Dale Walsh was still out there somewhere, and dead or alive, he was bound to turn up sooner or later.

Cage knew what he should do. He should get the heck out of town while the getting was good.

But he couldn't deny the situation he suddenly found himself in was more than a little exhilarating. The prospect of immersing himself in real police work again gave him the kind of adrenaline buzz he hadn't experienced since he'd left the team.

Could be that he'd been looking at this all wrong, he mused. Maybe everything that had happened to him in the last several hours wasn't divine retribution, but divine intervention. Maybe someone upstairs was trying to throw him a bone.

And as to those men from San Miguel who were after him—if they hadn't yet identified him, it wouldn't be long until they did. For all he knew, they could already have colleagues in Dallas looking for him.

Maybe hiding here, right under their noses, was his smartest move. They were hunting Cage Nichols, not a guy named Dale Walsh.

Rolling onto his side, Cage closed his eyes. For the time being at least, he decided to ignore that little niggling voice warning him that Grace Steele's dark, soulful eyes might be playing hell with his judgment.

THE FEATHER BED at Miss Nelda's was a little too soft for Grace's liking. She'd tossed and turned for hours, her thoughts ping-ponging back and forth between the terrible doubts she'd had earlier about her own sister and then that lusty little flutter she'd felt for Dale Walsh.

Finally, she managed to dismiss the first concern. No matter what Lily's grievances might be, she would never deliberately set out to hurt anyone, let alone her own sister. They'd grown apart over the years, but Grace knew that somewhere beneath that hard, jaded exterior was still the same caring, sensitive person who had once rescued every stray animal that had wandered onto the ranch.

But if Lily hadn't been at the top of those stairs, then who had Grace seen?

She wanted to believe the whole episode was just an unfortunate accident. Maybe she really had tripped on the rug.

But how to explain the sound that drew her attention on the landing? The glimpse of movement out of the corner of her eye? The feel of a hand on her back a split second before she went tumbling?

Could she have imagined all that?

Grace had always prided herself on having a level head on her shoulders, but she couldn't deny the house where her parents had been murdered still wreaked havoc on her nerves.

She'd never told anyone, but she'd once

suffered a severe panic attack when she'd found herself alone at the ranch. For what seemed an eternity, she'd remained paralyzed in her bedroom, unable to move, unable even to breathe. And then just like that, the spell ended and she'd never experienced anything like it again.

But maybe something similar had happened to her earlier. A different kind of panic attack. It made about as much sense as her sister—or anyone else—trying to kill her.

And as for her attraction to Dale Walsh, she could look to her more immediate past to explain her overreaction. Daniel Costa's betrayal had really done a number on her confidence. As a deputy director, he'd been responsible for bringing Grace into the TBI where she'd quickly become one of the hottest young agents in the Bureau. Her meteoric rise, at least in part, could be traced directly back to the strings she'd allowed Daniel to pull on her behalf.

Once their relationship turned personal, Grace had been a little too willing to ignore her persistent doubts about Daniel's integrity because a man in his position often had to make tough decisions. At least that was how she tried to justify turning a blind eye.

And then Daniel had thrown her under the bus, apparently without a moment's hesitation in order to save his own hide. That had stung. A lot. He'd wounded her pride, embarrassed her in front of her peers and derailed a very promising career. But worst of all, he'd made Grace doubt herself. How could a woman with a future as bright as hers have been so blindly stupid?

Grace had learned a hard lesson from that unseemly mess, and now she was determined to keep the stain of misconduct and bad judgment from touching her current position. She had a chance to start over here in Jericho Pass. It might be her only chance. She wasn't about to blow it.

So she was attracted to Dale Walsh. Big deal. Why make a mountain out of a molehill? It had been Grace's experience that the initial spark usually fizzled out pretty quickly after spending time in a man's company. She doubted Walsh would be an exception.

And if she couldn't manage to keep her personal life separate from her professional one after everything she'd been through in Austin, well, then, she had no business wearing a badge anyway.

Grace fluffed her pillow, rolled over and decided she was going to fall asleep right then and there if it killed her. She'd just drifted off when the creaking of the windmill awakened her.

Except…she wasn't at the ranch.

Her eyes flew open, but she remained still as she listened again for the sound.

There it was!

The creak came, not from a windmill, she realized, but from the settling of a floorboard beneath a stealthy footfall.

Grace was facing the balcony, and she saw a shadow outside the glass door. Sliding open the nightstand drawer, she removed her gun as she climbed out of bed and slipped quietly across the room. But by the time she got to the door, the shadow had moved on.

She put her ear to the glass and listened for footsteps. After a moment, she could pick out the steady creak of the floorboards as someone walked away from her room.

Twisting the latch, she eased back the door and stepped out on the balcony. Even in the dim lighting, she could easily pick out the silhouette of a man two rooms down from hers. He had his hand on the doorknob.

He must have sensed her presence because

his other hand went behind him, as if he were reaching for a weapon.

Grace drew a bead. "Freeze!"

His hand stilled, but his head slowly rotated to face her. "It's Dale Walsh, Sheriff."

He moved out of the shadows then and Grace caught her breath. He had on nothing but a pair of jeans and he carried nothing in his hands but an ice bucket.

Quickly, she dropped her weapon to her side. "Sorry. I heard a noise and came out to investigate."

He held up the ice bucket. "Just getting some ice. Sorry to disturb you."

"No, it's okay. I'm not usually so jumpy. Strange bed and all that…" She trailed off awkwardly.

For a moment, neither of them said anything else, and the waiting silence strangely excited Grace. She tried not to stare, but there he was right in front of her, all sunburned skin and blazing blue eyes. She couldn't help noticing that her earlier assessment had been right on the money. Despite his lean build, Dale Walsh did have some serious guns.

"I didn't know you were staying here," she finally said.

"I didn't know you were staying here, either."

As he propped a hand on the wall beside her, Grace suddenly became aware of her own bedtime attire—cotton pajama bottoms and a thin knit tank top that, even in the dimmest of lighting, would clearly reveal the outline of her breasts.

Hardly the outfit she would have favored for her second meeting with Dale Walsh.

She resisted the urge to cover herself with her arms, which of course would only call more attention to the area she wished to hide. "I only moved in today. I've been staying out at my family's ranch since I got back to town, but that didn't work out so well."

"I hear that. An hour or two at a time is about all I can take of my sister's constant chatter, and you don't even want to get me started on my mother."

"I'll take your sister's chatter over my sister's cold shoulder any day of the week," Grace said.

"Silence is golden," he said with a devastating grin. "I'll take that deal. Of course, I should warn you that my sister comes with strings attached. Namely, the jerk she's married to."

"Still sounds like a fair exchange to me."

"That bad, huh?"

"Right now it is. But…that's a subject for another day," Grace tried to say lightly. "It's late, and your ass is melting."

"My what?"

"Ice. Your ice is melting."

"So it is." He straightened, but he made no move to leave.

Instead, he just stood there looking down at her, making her feel as if she had all the poise of a thirteen- year-old. Grace couldn't remember the last time she'd felt so flustered and self-conscious. Even the review board hadn't torpedoed her composure this badly.

"Well…I guess I should go in and try to get some sleep before the alarm goes off," she said. "I'll see you in the morning at nine, right?"

"Yes, ma'am. Nine o'clock sharp."

She stepped through the door and turned the lock. Leaning a shoulder against the frame, she listened for Dale Walsh's retreating footsteps.

It took a moment, but finally she heard the telltale creak of the floorboards as he moved away from her room.

And then Grace let out a breath she hadn't even realized she was holding.

Holy moly, she thought.

Chapter Seven

Cage felt like a new man the next morning. Amazing what a little sleep could do for the morale.

The pain in his knee had eased up, too. He'd iced it the night before, and now, after another quick shower, he wrapped it with a pressure bandage he'd bought at the discount store.

After slipping on his new jeans and shirt—a white western cut with pearl snaps that he thought would help him blend in better, he tugged on his boots, grabbed his wallet and headed out to find some food.

Miss Nelda—or was the blonde Miss Georgina?—was cleaning shadow boxes with a feather duster when he came downstairs.

"Well, good morning," she said with a bright smile. "My, aren't you looking chipper? How did you sleep last night?"

"Not too bad," he said. "That poofy thing is like sleeping on a cloud."

"You do look mighty rested," she observed.

"And mighty hungry."

"We've put out fresh fruit and pastries in the dining room, but if you're looking for something a little more substantial, there's a diner across the street. And don't worry about hurting our feelings. Our nephew, Billy Don, owns the place and that poor boy needs all the help he can get. Not the sharpest knife in the drawer, if you get my drift."

Cage picked up a newspaper from a nearby chair. "Mind if I take this with me?"

"Not at all. Ask for the special," she said. "It's the best value on the menu."

"Thanks for the tip."

"Oh, any time, dear." She turned back to her dusting. "So, how long do you expect to be with us?"

Cage paused at the door. "I guess it all depends."

She gave him a sidelong glance. "On whether or not you hit it off with Grace?"

"Excuse me?"

She smiled at his surprise. "Oh, we all know why you're here. This is a small town, Mr. Walsh. Or should I call you Detective?

Word travels fast so I hope you don't have any deep, dark secrets." Her coy expression suggested that she might be actually hoping for the opposite.

"Nothing too terrible," he murmured.

"I'm not so sure I believe you, young man. You have a certain…*je ne sais quoi,* shall we call it?"

"*Je ne sais quoi.* That's a new one," Cage said, grinning.

"My first beau had that same mysterious air." She fluttered her hand in front of her as if trying to conjure that unnamed something. "I suppose that's why my father never trusted him. That, and the fact that he was a thief, a liar and a first-class scoundrel. Ran off with my dowry on our wedding day."

"If you ask me, ma'am, he must have been a first-class fool."

"Oh, my." She fanned herself with the feather duster. "You do have that certain something, don't you? I hope poor Grace knows what she's letting herself in for."

"Let's not get ahead of ourselves," Cage said. "She hasn't offered me the job, yet."

Miss Nelda peered at him over the feathers. "Who says I was talking about a job?"

"Well, I wouldn't know what else you'd be talking about, Miss Nelda."

She smiled appreciatively at the use of her name, and Cage was glad he'd gotten it right. "I'm sure you wouldn't. Just as I'm sure it escaped your attention how pretty our new sheriff is."

"Is she? I hadn't noticed."

"Of course, I much preferred her hair the way she used to wear it, but Grace has the kind of face that can overcome an unfortunate style. All the Steele girls are just lovely. It's such a shame that none of them has ever married. Unless you count Grace's elopement with that Nance boy, but that ended so quickly, hardly anyone around here even remembers it anymore."

There was an elopement in Sheriff Steele's past? Now that surprised Cage. Spontaneous and romantic weren't exactly the words that came to mind when he thought of her. She'd struck him as levelheaded and reserved, but then, the only thing he really knew about Grace Steele was that someone had put out a hit on her.

"I've always wondered if it had something to do with what happened to their parents," Miss Nelda mused.

"What did?" Cage had flashed back to the previous night and lost track of the conversation.

Now that Miss Nelda had brought up the subject of Grace Steele, he couldn't stop thinking about the way she'd looked out on that balcony, her eyes luminous in the dark and her hair all mussed and sexy. He liked the way her lips parted slightly when she smiled and the way she seemed so totally unaware of her hotness.

He liked a lot of things about Grace Steele, not the least of which was what he'd seen beneath those thin cotton pajamas. Soft, womanly curves...

"We were talking about why Grace and her sisters never married," Miss Nelda reminded him. "I was saying I think it must have something to do with their parents."

"Did they go through a bad divorce or something?"

"Divorce? Oh, dear me, no. Their parents were murdered at home while the two youngest girls were just down the hallway, hiding under their bed. Can you imagine how terrifying that must have been for them? A trauma like that is bound to have long-lasting effects."

Miss Nelda had brought him back to the present with a hard thud. Grace Steele's parents had been murdered and now someone wanted to kill her. Cage wasn't real big on coincidences, but they did happen. He didn't want to make too much of this.

"Was the killer ever found?" he asked.

"No, and for a while after it happened, folks around here spent some mighty uneasy nights. It was horrifying to think that someone in our midst, someone who might live just down the street or go to our same church, could be so evil as to kill innocent folks in cold blood." She shuddered as she went back to the shadow boxes. "It was a long time ago, but I don't mind telling you. I still sometimes have nightmares about it."

"What makes you think it wasn't just some stranger passing through?"

She stopped dusting. "There were…other incidents."

"What kind of incidents?"

Her eyes took on a faraway look, as if she had gone away for a moment to another time and place that wasn't so pleasant. She tried to shrug off the melancholy with a smile, but she seemed to have lost some of her luster. "It was all such a long time ago. Best not to dwell on the past, I always say."

Cage wondered about her sudden reticence. He wanted to hear more, but he didn't dare press her. Beneath the flirtatious smiles and coy glances, he had a feeling Miss Nelda was really quite fragile.

"You run on along to breakfast." She shooed him toward the door with the duster. "And if you see Billy Don, tell him Sister and I need him to come over and change some lightbulbs for us. I happened to notice on my walk last evening that one of the bulbs on the balcony is burned out." The mischievous sparkle was back in her eyes when she added, "We wouldn't want someone who might wander out there—for whatever reason—to trip and have a nasty fall, would we?"

THE DINER ACROSS THE STREET was the typical small-town greasy spoon—a plate-glass front, a long counter inside where men in work clothes sat hunched over steaming cups of coffee and a line of red vinyl booths by the window that allowed patrons a panoramic view of the parking lot.

The place wasn't crowded that morning so Cage had his choice of seats. He slid into one of the vinyl booths facing the front so that he could see the door. He'd also noted the exits and taken a quick survey of the customers. No one seemed to pay him the slightest attention except for the man in the booth behind him. And he only gave Cage a cursory glance before he resumed his cell phone conversation.

A skinny, freckle-faced redhead came over to take his order. She set a glass of ice water in front of him, then turned over the coffee cup on the table and filled it from the carafe she carried in her right hand.

"Do you need to look at a menu, hon, or do you already know what you want?" She sat the coffeepot on the table and pulled an order pad from the pocket of her apron.

"I'll take the special," Cage said.

She gave him a wink. "Good choice. Be right back."

As she turned toward the counter, the guy in the booth behind Cage said, "Hey, Kel, can I get some more coffee back here, babe?"

"I just gave you a refill. You got a hollow leg or something?" she teased.

"Sure do. You play your cards right, I might just show it to you sometime."

Oh, brother, Cage thought.

"No, *thank* you," the waitress said adamantly.

"Ah, now, baby, what's the matter? You don't want to see my hollow leg?"

"I don't want to see *any* of your legs, Jesse Nance."

"Since when?"

"Since your old lady came in here and chewed my butt out good just for talking to you. That woman is downright scary when she's mad. And they say redheads have tempers!"

"You know what else they say about redheads?"

"Oh, hush your mouth."

"Come on, darlin'," he cajoled. "Sookie's bark is way worse than her bite."

"Says you," the waitress grumbled. "What does she think about your ex being back in town?"

"You mean Gracie?" He gave a low laugh. "Sookie's got nothing to worry about there, that's for damn sure. The second happiest day of my life was when that girl packed her bags and left town."

"Second happiest? What's your first?"

"I'll let you know, sweetie."

"Yeah, you do that, Jesse."

Cage hadn't meant to eavesdrop, but once he heard the name Nance, he'd remembered his conversation with Miss Nelda. That was the name of the boy she'd said Grace Steele had eloped with.

Now Cage found himself just itching to turn around and get another look at the guy. His first impression was of an average-looking man with dark brown hair and a sun-burned face. And he also had about the lamest pickup lines Cage had ever heard. Hard to believe that kind of corn had ever worked on a sophisticated woman like Grace.

But, hey, Cage was no George Clooney, either. Who was he to pass judgment on the guy just because he'd once been married to Grace Steele?

The bells over the door sounded, drawing his attention to the man who'd just walked in.

Now there was a guy who could give Clooney a run for his money, Cage thought.

The newcomer was tall, trim and handsome—in a pampered sort of way—and the expensive suit he wore looked totally out of place amidst all the denim and khaki in the diner. Cage figured he must be from out of town, a businessman just passing through or something, but he sure seemed to know where he was going. Without hesitation, he strode down the aisle toward Cage's booth, bypassing his table for the one behind him.

Whoever he was, he set the redheaded waitress all atwitter. She was still standing at Nance's booth, and Cage heard her gush, "Oh, Mr. McKinney! Nice to see you…good morning! What can I get for you?"

"Nothing, thanks. I've already had my breakfast." And in a far superior establishment, his haughty tone seemed to imply.

"Not even coffee?"

"Nothing."

"Oh. Well…if you change your mind, just holler."

"I'll take my check," Jesse said peevishly, obviously not too keen on having his thunder stolen.

"Just hold your horses," the waitress told him.

When she saw Cage, she stopped short, grimaced, then mouthed, *Sorry,* evidently having forgotten all about him.

Cage unfolded the paper and thumbed through the pages, surprised to find nothing about the shooting. But then, it was a local paper and the editorials seemed more concerned about the dismal prospects of the Jericho Pass Bobcats than about any trouble on the border.

High school football used to be about the most important thing to him, too, but those days seemed a long time ago, Cage reflected as he refolded the paper and slid it aside.

Behind him, he heard the McKinney man say in an impatient tone, "Okay, Jesse, here I am. What's so all-fired important that you had to drag me away from my Rotary Club breakfast?"

"I'll order you something here," Nance offered. "Anything you want."

"I'm not in the mood for a heart attack so I'll take a pass on the grease," McKinney said snidely. "Tell me what this is about so I can get on with my day."

"Okay. I'll just put it right out there, then," Nance said. "There's a rumor going around town that you've been sniffing around the Steele place."

"So?"

"I thought you and me had a deal."

"I repeat, so?"

Nance paused. "Are you really interested in buying that place or is this just one of your tricks?"

"I have no idea what you're talking about," McKinney said.

"Sookie thinks this is just a ploy on your part to drive down my asking price."

"If that's what Sookie thinks, then she's dumber than she looks," McKinney said bluntly. "I'm perfectly willing to honor my original offer. You're the one dragging your feet."

"I told you, I have to clear up that little deed problem first."

"Then do it."

"It's not as easy as you make it sound. I have to be real careful how I handle this."

"Just stop whining and take care of the problem, for God's sake."

"I'm working on it. But I need a little more time."

"How much time?"

"A few more days."

"Forty-eight hours," McKinney told him. "And I warn you, if I have to get involved in this again, the aggravation is going to cost you. Maybe you ought to see what Sookie has to say about that?"

McKinney got up and strode past Cage's booth to the door. Behind him, Cage heard Jesse Nance scramble to his feet to follow him out. The two men continued their discussion in the parking lot. From McKinney's expression and Nance's frenzied gestures, the conversation was getting more heated by the moment.

The redhead brought over Cage's breakfast, drawing his attention momentarily away from the window.

"Sorry for the delay," she said with an apologetic smile.

"No problem." As she topped off his coffee, Cage said, "That man out there...the tall one. He looks familiar, but I can't place him."

"Oh, that's Colt McKinney."

Cage could have sworn she actually let out a dreamy little sigh when she said his name.

"I'm pretty sure we've met before," Cage said. "Does he live around here?"

"You've probably seen his picture in the paper. He's kind of Cochise County's version of Donald Trump. Except *way* cuter."

"Big shot, huh?"

"Big, big shot. His family owns most of the land and businesses around here. They were cattle ranchers back when there was good money in it, but nowadays, Colt dabbles in a little bit of everything, including politics."

"What about the guy with him? Are they business partners?"

She laughed out loud at that. "Not hardly. Jesse Nance is just about the biggest loser you're ever likely to run across. Never worked an honest day in his life. He's been living off the money his old man left him for years, but he's flat busted now. What little he had left, Sookie Truesdale ran through when they hooked up. Talk about high maintenance," she said with a disdainful sniff.

"Takes cold hard cash to keep a woman like that happy," Cage said, as if he knew Sookie personally.

"Yeah, well, the only thing Jesse's got left to his name is that broken-down old ranch." She leaned down and lowered her voice. "I'll give you three guesses as to why Sookie hasn't already dumped his ass."

Cage shrugged.

"I hear Colt's made him an offer on his land. And you can bet Sookie's gonna get her paws on as much of that cash as she can before she splits."

The waitress straightened and gave Cage a wink. "Anything else I can get for you, hon?"

Chapter Eight

Cage decided that conducting a stealth investigation in Jericho Pass might be a little like shooting fish in a barrel. He didn't need to be all clever and sly to ferret out information. All he had to do was ask a few questions and then stand back.

If everyone in that town liked to talk as much as Miss Nelda and the redheaded waitress, Cage shouldn't have too much difficulty finding out everything he needed to know in fairly short order.

Whether they were just trying to be friendly or whether there was a self-important aspect to their openness, he had no idea. What he did know was that in less than an hour's time, he'd already learned about the murder of Grace Steele's parents and her elopement with Jesse Nance. He knew that Colt McKinney was the town bigwig and Grace's ex was the town loser, and the two of them were cooking up a deal together. McKinney had made an offer on Nance's ranch, but Nance had a problem with the deed. A problem he intended to care of.

The only thing Cage hadn't found out yet was who had paid a hit man five thousand dollars up front to come to town and take care of Grace.

But he was closer than he had been last night.

Something about that deal with Colt McKinney and Jesse Nance had set off a few alarm bells for Cage, and he was still thinking about their conversation when he walked into the sheriff's station a little while later. Sam Dickerson greeted him with another goofy grin.

"How's that Caddy holding up in all this West Texas grit?"

"So far, so good," Cage said. "Is Sheriff Steele in? I'm supposed to be meeting her here at nine."

"She's on a conference call right now. She'll give a holler when she's through. Since you've got a little time to kill, why don't I give you the grand tour?"

Cage shrugged. "Sure, why not?"

He followed Sam around the station, nodding politely, and occasionally shaking hands when he was introduced to the staff. Deputy Dickerson seemed to have an endless repertoire of stories and anecdotes about everyone in the department, and Cage soon learned to laugh in all the right places without really paying much attention to what was being said.

The deputy insisted on showing him the whole nine yards of the operation, including the interrogation room, the communications room, the copy room, the break room, the map-lined conference room, and the holding cells in the back. A shoulder-high wall separated the four desks that made up Criminal Investigations from the rest of the department, and Dickerson saved that area for last.

Two of the desks were nearly covered over with case files, reports and myriad forms, while a third seemed to have the same amount of paperwork but in a more orderly configuration. The fourth desk had only the usual office paraphernalia of paper clips, staplers and pen holders.

"That'll be your desk right there if you decide to take the job," Sam said. "It's nice and clean right now, but give it a day or two and it'll look more like that." He pointed to the mile-high stacks of file folders.

Cage wasn't impressed. His old desk hadn't looked much different. Every cop in the country was probably overworked to a certain degree, especially the ones that investigated crimes against persons. The red tape alone was staggering.

"Cruz caught a call first thing this morning, and it's Mosley's day off. But Lily should be around here somewhere," Dickerson said. "If you have any questions, I'm sure she'd be happy to answer them. Just hang tight and I'll go see if I can find her."

After he was gone, Cage glanced down at an open folder on the third desk. It was an autopsy report from the county medical examiner.

"Hey! What the *hell* do you think you're doing?"

Cage looked up.

"Yeah, you. I'm talking to you. Take a step back, slick."

The woman bounding toward him couldn't have weighed much more than a hundred and ten pounds soaking wet, but she had a bulldozer quality about her that would probably make most people think twice before getting in her way.

"You got business here or you just plain nosy?" she demanded. A thick, black braid fell over her shoulder as she leaned across the desk to close the folder.

"Both," he said with a grin.

She glowered until his grin faded.

"Sorry. I was just waiting around to see Sheriff Steele," he told her.

"Then why don't you go wait in her office instead of mine?"

"Uh, I think Deputy Dickerson wanted me to meet you."

"Oh, he did, did he?" Her gray eyes swept over him. "And just who are you?"

"Dale Walsh."

One brow lifted slightly. "Well, well, well. The infamous Detective Walsh finally graces us with his presence."

"Why infamous?"

"Because Charlie Dickerson built you up so much, I was beginning to think you were nothing more than a myth. Or a figment of his imagination. But here you are." She gave him another quick appraisal. "Not quite what I had in mind."

"Sorry to disappoint."

"Not half as sorry as I am," she muttered.

The mocking quality of her voice was a nice accessory to her derision, Cage decided. This woman was definitely a pistol.

"I didn't catch your name," he said.

"Lily Steele."

"Are you—"

"No relation to our illustrious sheriff," she said before he had a chance to finish his question. "It's just an unfortunate coincidence that we share the same last name."

"Why unfortunate?"

"Have you met her?" Lily's taunting gaze slid past him. "Speak of the devil."

Cage turned to find Sheriff Steele striding toward them.

"Sorry you had to wait," she said. "I see you've met my sister."

He turned back to Lily who merely shrugged as she plopped down in her chair and reached for a folder.

"I just got a call about a situation out in the county," Grace said. "You want to ride along?"

Cage shrugged. "Sure, if I won't be stepping on anyone's toes."

"We're not that territorial around here," Grace said. Then her gaze dropped to her sister. "For the most part."

"What's going on?" Lily asked.

"A body was found just off Tombstone Road, east of Red Rock Canyon."

"That's close to Jesse Nance's place."

Something flickered in Lily's eyes, a look of fear, Cage thought. "It's not…Jesse, is it?"

Grace looked surprised. "Why would you think that?"

Lily glanced away. "Because you said the body was found near his place. And we both know Jesse can't keep himself out of trouble."

"Well, it's not him," Grace said. "Nobody seems to know who this guy is yet." As she turned toward Cage, her jacket swung open, revealing the star-shaped badge clipped to her gun belt.

Cage could also see the outline of her bra through the cotton shirt she wore, but he tried to pretend that he couldn't. As he averted his gaze, he saw that Lily was staring up at him. His attention hadn't lingered on Grace's chest for more than a split second, but it was enough for Lily to notice and give him a smirk.

"Are you ready to go?" Grace asked.

Cage nodded. "Let's hit it."

"Hey, Dale?"

Reluctantly, he turned back to Lily.

She smiled innocently. "So, are you going to be around for a while?"

"Looks that way."

"Some of us are going over to the Blue Moon tonight to have some drinks and shoot a little pool. Why don't you drop in if nothing better pops up?" Her gaze shifted to Grace, then back to him and she smirked again.

"Thanks. Maybe I will."

"I'd invite you, too, Grace, but I'm sure you'd feel out of place among us peons."

"Ouch," Cage said under his breath as he and Grace turned to leave. "I see what you mean about the cold shoulder."

"She's been that way for as long as I can remember," Grace said with a shrug, but Cage could tell that she was bothered by her sister's attitude. "I've given up trying to figure her out."

"Must make working for the same department a little awkward."

"Believe me, that was a *big* consideration before I decided to come back here."

Outside, the sun was blistering. Heat rose in waves from the asphalt parking lot, and Grace pulled off her jacket and tossed it onto the seat between them before climbing into the truck.

"Listen," Cage said. "I need to come clean with you about something."

She gave him a curious glance. "I'm listening."

"It's about that guy Lily mentioned. Jesse Nance."

Something flickered in her eyes, but her expression remained carefully neutral. "What about him?"

"I know that he's your ex."

"Don't tell me people are talking about that. It was a hundred years ago." She put the truck in gear and pressed down on the accelerator. The vehicle rocketed forward before Cage had a chance to fasten his seat belt.

She shot him a glance. "Who told you? Lily?"

"Miss Nelda mentioned it."

"Busybody," Grace muttered, and Cage wasn't certain at first to whom she was referring.

She said nothing else for a moment as she ran a hand through her dark hair. "Miss Nelda's a sweet old woman, but she can't seem to mind her own business. I don't know what I was thinking, moving into that boarding house."

"For what it's worth, I don't think she meant any harm. She seems fond of you."

Grace nodded. "Yeah, I know. And I've always liked her, too. She and Miss Georgina can be a real hoot, but I have to worry about my public image. I know that sounds trite, but to do this job right, I need to maintain an air of respectability."

"I understand."

"A county sheriff is an authority figure, and when you're my age and a woman to boot, you've already got two strikes against you. The last thing I need is people gossiping about me."

He put up a hand. "You're preaching to the choir, here."

She chewed on her lip. "So… What else did she say about me?"

He gave her a doubtful look. "You really want to know?"

"Sure, why not? I may as well know what people are saying about me behind my back. Forewarned is forearmed, right?"

Cage glanced out the window. They'd quickly left the town limits behind, and the only thing he could see for miles was scrub brush, yucca and the occasional pumpjack silhouetted against the horizon. The feeling of isolation in that wide, vast openness still took him by surprise.

He turned back to Grace. "She told me that your parents had been murdered when you were just a kid. She said you and Lily were home when it happened."

Grace stared straight ahead without comment.

"Sorry," he said. "I didn't mean to bring up such a painful subject."

"No, it's okay. I asked you to tell me. And it's not so painful that I can't talk about it or stand to hear about it. It happened a long time ago. Sometimes it almost seems like it was just a bad dream. Something you think about in passing at times, and then you just get on with your life."

Brave words, but Cage saw her grip tighten on the steering wheel.

"How old were you when it happened?"

A trickle of sweat ran down the side of her face, and she swiped it away as she tucked her hair behind her ears. "Ten. Lily was six. I remember that something woke me up that night. I thought it was the windmill at first. It used to creak so loudly that you could hear it for miles, it seemed. It's a sound I never forgot, even after I'd been away from here for a long, long time."

"Sounds are like smells," Cage said. "They can stay with you for years, trigger memories you didn't even know you had." His trigger had once been the smell of freshly mown grass. That scent always took him straight back to his high school football years.

Nowadays it was the smell of fresh paint. That was what he remembered most about the night he'd been shot. Not the pain or the fear or the metallic taste of blood in his mouth, but the acrid fumes in the house where a man had held his wife and two kids hostage for hours.

"After a while, I realized that what I heard was footsteps on the stairs," Grace said. "When he got to the top, he stopped and just…stood there for the longest time. It was like he was waiting for something."

"Maybe he was just trying to get his bearings."

"Maybe." She scowled at the road. "I don't know why I didn't call out. Maybe I was too scared. I woke Lily up and she and I crawled under her bed. We stayed there until I was sure he was gone."

"You didn't see anything?"

"Just his boots in the hallway."

"What about a car?"

She shook her head. "I didn't even think to look."

"Any suspects?"

"My parents had no enemies, and we certainly weren't rich so there was no reason for someone to think there'd be cash in the house."

"Was anything taken?"

"Nothing."

"How did he get in?"

Cage thought for a moment she wouldn't answer. Then she drew a breath and slowly released it. "I left the front door unlocked."

Now it was Cage who remained silent.

"I'd left my bicycle out in the driveway and my dad was afraid my sister, Rachel, would hit it if she came home early from her sleepover. She used to do that sometimes. Even after she was old enough to drive, she never liked spending the night away from home, which is strange, because after she left for college, she never came back."

"And you're sure you left the door unlocked when you came back in?"

"I must have. I was the last one in that night. And there was no sign of a forced entry. Just that unlocked front door."

"You were only ten years old," he said softly.

"I know."

"You can't blame yourself."

"I don't."

But in spite of the denial, Cage was willing to bet that unlocked door had tormented her for years.

"What about fingerprints or tire tracks?

There must have been some kind of trace evidence."

"There was nothing."

"There was something," Cage said. "There's always something left behind. It just didn't get found."

Grace shrugged. "That was twenty-three years ago. We didn't have the kind of forensic technology we have these days. And even now, we both know it's never as easy as those CSI shows make it seem. Especially in a place like Cochise County."

"Miss Nelda said the authorities were convinced it was someone local because of other incidents that happened. She was kind of vague about that."

"She must have been talking about the other murders," Grace said, and she gave him another quick glance.

"What other murders?"

"Ellen and John Lomax. They were ranchers, too. They were found murdered on their kitchen floor the year before my parents were killed."

"Same M.O.?"

"Similar, except they were killed in the middle of the day. They'd just sat down to lunch. The table was set for three and there was still food on the plates and coffee in the cups. Whoever it was, they had invited him to sit down and eat with them. Their sixteen-year-old daughter got sick at school that day and came home early. She must have seen the killer. Her truck was found in a ravine a few miles from the ranch. She was headed back toward town when her vehicle was forced off the road. She got out to run, but he caught her and shot her in the head. Left her right where she fell. If he was able to do that to her…" Grace swiped another strand of hair from her forehead. "I've often wondered why he spared Lily and me when he must have known we were there that night."

"Even a monster might have a hard time killing two little girls in cold blood."

"He didn't seem to have a problem killing the Lomax girl."

"She was older and that was in the heat of the moment. And it is possible he didn't know you were hiding under the bed."

"If it was someone local, then he had to have known we were somewhere in the house. Just as he knew that Jenny Lomax would be in school that day."

"And the police were convinced it was the same perpetrator in your parents' case?"

"The M.O. was close enough that it seemed likely."

"What did the ballistics reports show?"

"They weren't a match, but that doesn't mean anything. Almost everyone in Cochise County owns more than one gun."

Something about all this was starting to bother Cage. "Let's just assume it *was* someone local. Someone that still lives around here. Have you ever considered that your return might be making him sweat a little?"

Grace frowned. "Why would he be worried about me? He's gotten away with five murders for this long. Besides, if he thought there was a chance I'd seen something that night, he could have killed me a long time ago."

"Like I said, whacking a kid might not be so easy, even for him."

"You're forgetting about my sister," Grace said. "Lily's lived here all her life. If he's concerned I'll remember something, why hasn't he been worried about her all this time?"

"Put it this way," Cage said. "If you had to rely on a six-year-old or a ten-year-old witness, which one would you choose?"

"Yeah, I guess. But like I said, this guy has gotten away with murder for twenty-three years. You think he's going to risk his freedom now by coming after me on the off chance I might remember something?"

"All it takes is the right sound," Cage said. "Or a smell."

Grace shook her head. "If I was going to remember something about that night, I would have done so by now. There's just nothing to remember because I didn't see anything. Besides, the killer could already be dead for all we know. Or in prison for another crime."

"That's certainly possible."

She turned and studied him for a moment. "Why are you so interested in all this?"

He shrugged. "I'm a cop. The notion of a killer going free all this time goes against my grain." *And somebody around here wants you dead, lady.*

"You don't think it goes against mine? We're talking about my parents here. I've dreamed about catching the person or persons responsible for as long as I can remember. It's the reason I entered law enforcement in the first place. But I'm a realist. In the past two years alone, the Mexican police have reported over five thousand— that's *five thousand*—gangland-style killings, and that violence is starting to spill across the border. That's where I have to direct this department's resources and manpower. I can't indulge myself in trying to solve a twenty-three-year-old homicide case. Not even when it's as close to me as this one. My duty is to protect the citizens of Cochise County to the best of my ability, and that's exactly what I intend to do."

Admirable, Cage thought. But luckily, he wasn't hampered by such noble constraints.

They'd been traveling south since they'd left Jericho Pass and the low walls of an arroyo eventually gave way to a high bluff that ran parallel to the road.

Grace nodded toward the window. "Red Rock Canyon," she told him.

She'd slipped on her sunglasses earlier and now she pulled them down her nose so that she could study the striated formations over the rims. "There's a legend about this place. One of the south-facing walls has a pictograph of a giant thunderbird which some say marks the tomb of a monstrous winged predator who once fed on the tribes that lived in this area. On moonless nights, the lights that can be seen moving through the canyon are the souls of his victims, trying to find a passage to heaven. Others say the thunderbird guards a secret door behind which is a fortune in gold."

"Nothing like a good legend to lighten the mood," Cage said. "I've always been a sucker for ghost stories."

"Then you'll want to see Willow Springs," she said.

"What's Willow Springs?"

"A ghost town about twenty miles from here. But if you want to visit it, I wouldn't advise taking your car. The trail is pretty rugged. You'll need a four-wheel drive."

"I'll keep that in mind," he said. "So, what's the scoop on that place?"

"It was once a thriving mercury-mining town and now there's nothing left but deserted mine shafts, a few crumbling buildings and the ghost of the murdered sheriff who still roams the streets, trying to protect the town from the marauders who gunned him down in a spectacular shoot-out."

"Sounds like a Clint Eastwood movie."

"I'm sure it is," she said with a smile, and then she sobered.

Up ahead, two squad cars and a county coroner's SUV were pulled to the side of the road. Cage felt that little jolt in his gut that he used to get before every mission.

Just like old times, he thought and for a moment he sat there and savored the feeling, no matter how fleeting, of being back in the game.

Chapter Nine

About a hundred yards off the road, two uniformed deputies and two men in plain clothes stood gazing down at something on the ground. When they saw Grace, one of them raised a hand and waved her over.

"That's Raymond Cruz," she said, referring to the taller of the two men in jeans. "He's one of our detectives. The guy standing next to him is the county coroner, Ellis Lovejoy."

"Great name for a coroner," Cage said.

"Isn't it?"

As they neared the crime scene, Cage could hear the sputter of radio transmissions and the sound stirred about a million memories. Different town, different cops, different scenery for sure. But the old thrill was still there.

He hung back, not wanting to overstep his bounds, but he was itching to get a look at the victim. The deputies and Detective Cruz stepped back to make room for Grace, and she stood for a moment, gazing down at the ground with them. Then she took off her sunglasses and knelt beside the body.

"Who called it in?"

"A couple of teenagers on four-wheelers spotted him," Cruz told her. "They left tracks all over the damn place."

"I don't guess we know who he is yet, do we?"

"We don't have a name, but Mac here thinks the guy may be related to Cecelia Suarez."

Cage saw Grace's head jerk up. "Colt McKinney's housekeeper?"

Cruz nodded. "He says he saw them together one night at the Blue Moon. Cecelia said he was her brother."

"When was this, Mac?"

One of the deputies shifted closer to Grace. "Couple weeks ago, maybe closer to three. I saw them arguing out in the parking lot. Looked like the guy was starting to get out of line so I went over to break things up and make sure Cecelia was okay. She just laughed it off and said her brother couldn't hold his liquor. She called him *la endeble,* which didn't sit too well with him."

"Did you hear his name?"

"She never called him by name, and I didn't really get that good a look at him. It was pretty dark in the parking lot and I didn't have my flashlight with me. But I'm pretty sure this is the same guy."

"How sure is pretty sure?"

"I'm not willing to swear on it, but you don't see a scar like that very often."

"Has anyone talked to Cecelia yet?" Grace asked. "We'll need to get her over to the morgue for an ID."

"I'll swing by there on my way back to the station," Cruz said. "Unless you want to do it. Might be easier coming from a woman."

He didn't seem to mean any disrespect by the comment, and Grace didn't appear to take offense. She glanced up at the coroner. "Any guess as to the time of death?"

"Based on algor mortis, I'd say at least ten hours, but it gets pretty cool out here at night." He shrugged, which seemed to mean, *Your guess is as good as mine.*

Grace stood and glanced over her shoulder at Cage. "Come take a look. Tell me what you think."

The other cops dispersed as Cage moved up beside Grace. The victim lay facedown in the dirt, hands tied behind his back, long black hair matted with blood.

Grace handed Cage a pair of gloves and he snapped them on as he knelt. His hand poised over the victim's head, he said, "Mind if I take a look?"

"Be my guest."

He parted the matted hair until he could see the entrance wound at the back of the man's skull.

"Looks about the size of a .357 Magnum."

"Yep, that's what it looks like all right," the coroner agreed. "But we won't know for sure until we dig that slug out."

The victim was facing away from Cage, and he moved around to the other side, this time lifting the hair away from the man's features.

He was Hispanic, early twenties with a wicked-looking scar that curved around his throat. Cage had seen that scar before. He knew who this man was.

He was the guy who'd gone out the bathroom window in San Miguel, leaving his wife behind to be slaughtered with all the others.

It appeared that someone else was being dealt a little divine retribution, Cage thought grimly.

"SHERIFF STEELE! YOU BETTER come take a look at this," one of the deputies hollered. He was standing at the base of a rock outcropping that looked a bit like that winged monster Grace had told Cage about earlier.

This time Cage didn't wait for an invitation. He picked his way through the rugged terrain behind her.

At first he thought the mound of loose stones was a grave. Then he saw the candles and the grim reaper figurines, and he glanced over at Grace. Her face had gone almost white.

"What is this?"

"It's an altar," she said in a clipped tone.

"What's it doing out here?"

"The same thing he is." She nodded toward the corpse. "Paying tribute to *Santa Muerte*. The patron saint of death."

Cage's gaze narrowed as he watched her. He could tell she was upset and trying very hard not to show it to everyone in attendance. "Are you saying this is a ritual killing instead of a gangland hit?"

"I'm saying it could be both," Grace said. "Probably is both. The worship of *Santa Muerte* is a cult that's become popular with a certain criminal element in Mexico, especially the enforcers who work for the drug cartels.

It has its roots in Santeria, but the followers have come to be known as *narcosatánicos*."

She bent and picked up one of the figurines. Even under the burning sun, the empty-eyed deity looked eerie and haunting. Somehow evil.

Grace ran her gloved finger along the curve of the scythe. "If you go across the border, you see these things all over the place, especially in Nuevo Laredo. Shops, cemeteries, graffiti on city walls. Sometimes you even see it on the drug runners' bulletproof SUVs."

"That's pretty brazen."

"Until now, our main concern was the danger of abduction posed to American citizens crossing over the border, but then sheriff's deputies in Laredo started finding evidence of ritualistic ceremonies in stash houses that they raided. Gruesome stuff—blood-filled bowls, animal sacrifices, you name it."

She tossed the figurine back on the makeshift altar. "What we're seeing is a culture of death," she said. "And it's right here in our own backyard."

THEY BOTH SAID VERY LITTLE on the way back to town. Grace was too preoccupied—and worried—by what they'd found at the crime scene to try and make small talk.

Dale seemed distracted, too. His head was turned toward the window, but somehow Grace didn't think he was watching the scenery.

"Does this change things for you?" she finally asked.

It took him a moment to respond. He turned, but only to stare out the windshield. "It changes things," he said. "It changes everything, but not in the way you mean."

She frowned at his vagueness. "What do you mean?"

He looked at her then, and his blue eyes seemed to burn right through her. Grace felt a quiver in the pit of her stomach. She wanted to look away, but found that she couldn't.

"That guy back there…"

"Yeah? What about him?"

"He—"

Whatever he'd been about to tell her was cut short by the sound of a shotgun blast a split second before the back windshield in the truck disintegrated. Glass from the exploding window peppered Grace's arm and the side of her face, and she jumped, as much from the shock as the pain.

"Get down!" she screamed as the truck veered off the road and another blast took off the side mirror.

Grace slid down in the seat, contorting herself to keep her head below the rear window opening while flooring the accelerator. Out of the corner of her eye, she saw Dale twist in the seat to get a look out the back.

"It's coming from the top of the canyon," he yelled.

Grace headed straight for a stand of mesquite bushes. It wasn't much cover, but it was the only thing around for miles.

As she swung the truck around and slammed on the brakes, Dale opened the door and jumped out. The entire front seat was covered in glass, and Grace could feel the chunks slice into her skin like a cheese grater as she slid across to the passenger side and rolled out behind him.

Keeping her head down, she made her way toward the front of the vehicle where Dale hunkered in the dirt, peering around the bumper.

"I saw a flash," he said. "Just to the right of that juniper tree."

Grace gripped her gun as she eased around him to have a look.

"What's the quickest way to the top?" he asked.

"There's a trail about a mile down the road."

"He'll be long gone by then." He took another peek around the bumper. "Cover me," he said.

"What?"

"Cover me."

Before Grace could protest, he darted around the truck and sprinted toward the canyon.

"Idiot," she muttered as she watched him zigzag across the open expanse.

Buckshot tore through the scrub brush at his feet, kicking up trails of tiny dirt clouds, and for a moment as he staggered, Grace thought he might have been hit.

She got off several rounds before a spray of slugs pinged across the side of the truck, ripping through the metal as though it were tin foil and forcing her back behind the wheel well in shock.

Grace's heart was pumping so hard, she could feel the beat in her temples. But her hand was still steady, thank God. She waited a split second, then popped up over the hood and started firing. She didn't stop until Dale reached the base of the canyon where he could take cover. Then she retreated behind the truck and slid down in the dirt, her back against the tire as she reloaded.

She wiped sweat from her eyes and her hand came back bloody. For some reason, the story she'd told Dale earlier about Willow Springs popped into her head, and she felt an unexpected kinship with the sheriff whose ghost still wandered those deserted streets, waiting for his final showdown.

THE BLAST OF BUCKSHOT was so close that Cage was momentarily rattled and he lost his footing as he dodged and twisted through an obstacle course of scrub brush, prickly pear and cacti. As his knee gave way, he thought for sure he was going down, but somehow he managed to stay on his feet and now the sound of gunfire behind him spurred him on. Grace was giving him some cover.

By the time he reached the base of the canyon, he was breathing hard and swearing. And he had a wrenching pain in his leg that started at the kneecap and shot all the way up his thigh.

What the hell had he been thinking? He couldn't handle a climb that rugged.

But climb he did, his feet slipping and sliding in the loose shale. The narrow canyon held the heat like a kiln, and by the time Cage reached the top, he was panting and sweating and his knee had gone almost numb, which helped him at that moment but he knew he would pay for it later.

He didn't bother with cover now. No shots had been fired for the past several minutes and Cage had only been halfway to the top when he heard the sound of a retreating ATV. He kept going anyway, and when he made it to the top, he gave Grace the all-clear sign before he scoured the ground for shell casings and tire tracks.

She came up after him, and as her head popped up over the canyon rim, Cage saw the thin rivulets of blood that ran down the side of her face where she'd been pelted by the exploding glass.

"Find anything?"

Cage was still poking around in the dirt. "ATV tracks," he said. "Looks like a four-wheeler."

She walked over to have a look, and he handed her a handkerchief. "You're bleeding."

"Thanks." When she reached for the handkerchief, he noticed that her hand was all cut up, too.

"Are you okay?"

She turned her hand over and briefly examined the wounds. "Yeah, it's just scratches. Looks a lot worse than it is."

"You'll need to put something on them. You don't want them to get infected."

She didn't seem too concerned as she squatted in the dirt to examine the tire tracks. "He must have gone down the trail on the other side," she said.

"Does anyone live around here?"

Grace stood and wound the handkerchief around her bleeding hand. He could see dots of blood already showing through the linen.

"There's a ranch about a mile and a half north of here."

"Who owns it?"

She glanced at him. "Jesse Nance."

"Do you know if he has a four-wheeler?"

"Everyone around here has a four-wheeler," she said. "Ranchers use them nowadays instead of horses. But what on earth makes you think that Jesse would open fire on us like that?"

"Ex-husbands have been known to bear grudges," Cage said with a shrug.

She laughed. "Not after this many years. We were only married three months."

"Well, somebody's got a beef with you,"

Cage said. "Unless you think that ambush was random, and I'm hard-pressed to believe that it was. Whoever was up here had a clear view of the road and the Sheriff's Department emblem on the side of your truck. The shooter knew exactly who he was firing on."

"Yeah, maybe."

"No maybe about it," Cage said. "Somebody was trying to kill you."

"Oh, yeah?" Grace gave him a strange, searching look. "How do we know they weren't firing at you?" she asked, before she turned and started down the canyon.

Chapter Ten

Grace did not think for a moment that Jesse Nance had been up on that ridge firing down on them. For one thing, he hadn't seemed all that cut up when their marriage ended, so she highly doubted he'd been carrying a grudge all these years.

And for another, he just wasn't the type. He had his faults, no one knew that better than Grace. The Jesse she remembered was lazy, selfish and irresponsible, and his lack of ambition was only exceeded by his lack of scruples. But he'd had his limits and Grace just couldn't see him being involved in anything truly dastardly.

Still, his ranch was the only one for miles around, and the body had been found at the edge of his property. At the very least, Grace needed to find out if he'd witnessed any unusual or suspicious activity in the desert lately.

She pulled up in front of the house and sat for a moment, just staring through the windshield. Boy, did that place take her back.

In its time, the Nance Ranch must have been something. Grace could well imagine the lavish barbecues at roundup, the sound of music and laughter echoing across the desert, the rustle of silk skirts on a makeshift dance floor beneath the stars. But by the time she and Jesse had become friends, the Nance family fortune had dwindled and the ranch was already in a sad state of decline.

After his father died, the upkeep had proven too much for his mother's salary as a nurse. Jesse and his sister each had trust funds, but they couldn't touch the money until they turned twenty-five. Once the family's savings had been depleted, there'd been no extra cash for anything other than the most necessary repairs, and for as long as Grace could remember, the house had been nothing more than a shadow of its former glory.

But she'd always loved coming here, and had never paid much mind to the shabbiness. She, Jesse and Colt McKinney had been inseparable all through junior high and high school. They'd spent most of their free time out here riding horses and four-wheelers and swimming in a little creek near Red Rock Canyon.

Sometime after her sixteenth birthday, Grace and Jesse had paired off, and Colt quit coming around so much. But Grace had still spent every waking moment at the Nances, and Jesse's mother, Aggie, had doted on her. Jesse had once told Grace that the reason his mother had taken their elopement so well was because she already loved Grace like a daughter, and thought she just might be the only thing that could save Jesse from a life of sloth and debauchery.

Aggie Nance had died the same year Grace left town, and she still regretted not coming back for the funeral.

"You okay?" Dale asked softly.

"Yeah. Let's get this over with."

As they climbed out of the truck, a woman who looked barely out of her teens came out on the porch. She was dressed in short shorts and cowboy boots, and the crop top she wore revealed an expanse of smooth, tanned skin. Her face was narrow, the nose perfectly shaped, her silky hair fastened in a high ponytail that swayed when she moved. Her eyes were blue, not vivid cobalt like Dale's, but a pale aquamarine.

As Grace approached the porch, the woman watched her with all the friendliness and warmth of a pit viper.

Grace dipped her chin. "Morning. I'm Sheriff Steele—"

"I know who you are." Insolence dripped like molasses off the woman's drawl as her gaze ran up and down Grace's dusty clothes. "You're a lot older than I thought you'd be."

Grace wished that she could say the woman was a lot younger than she'd expected, but she figured it was Jesse's natural inclination to gravitate to someone more in keeping with his maturity level.

Not to mention someone with those legs. They looked about a mile long between the top of her boots and the bottom of her shorts. And not so much as a ripple of cellulite anywhere that Grace could see.

On closer inspection, Grace decided the woman was a little older than she'd first thought. She might have been all of twenty-three.

"I don't believe I've had the pleasure," Grace said.

The young woman hesitated a split second,

as if working it out in her head whether or not she should give Grace her name. "Sookie Truesdale."

"That's an unusual name."

"I'm named after my grandmother."

"Hey, so am I. I guess that gives us a thing or two in common," Grace said, trying to break the ice.

"Well, we've both been with Jesse Nance," Sookie said. "But I don't reckon that gives either one of us any bragging rights."

"Speaking of Jesse, is he home?"

"Nah uh."

"Do you know where I can find him? Or when he'll be back?"

"What do I look like, his secretary?" Sookie's gaze moved past Grace to where Dale stood by the truck. "He a deputy or something? I haven't seen him around before."

"He's new."

Sookie gave an appreciative nod. "Well, I always said this place could use some fresh man candy. And he looks pretty munchable to me." She tore her eyes off Dale and refocused on Grace. "There's blood on the side of your face. What did you do, get in a fight or something?"

"Cat scratched me," Grace said.

"Cat do that to your truck, too?"

"It was a big cat."

Sookie smirked as she lifted a hand and smoothed back a strand of hair. For the first time, Grace noticed that the woman's face was slightly flushed, as if she'd been exerting herself, or had just come in from the heat. "What do you want with Jesse?"

"I just need to ask him a few questions."

"Is he in some kind of trouble?"

"Not so far as I know. This is strictly routine." Grace propped a foot on the bottom step.

"Well, like I said, I don't know when he'll be back."

"Maybe I could ask you a question or two then," Grace said. "Have you seen any strangers around here lately?"

Sookie nodded toward the truck. "You mean besides Pretty over there?"

"Yeah, besides him."

She lifted a shoulder.

"Does that mean yes or no?"

"It means I don't rightly remember at the moment."

"Well, do you *remember* if Jesse was home last night?" Grace asked in a slightly goading tone.

The blue eyes narrowed as Sookie folded

her arms across her chest. "I thought you said he wasn't in any trouble."

"He's not. But there has been some trouble out by the canyon," Grace told her. "I'd like to know if he saw anybody out there last night."

"I wouldn't know," Sookie said. "I spent the night in town with a girlfriend. Sarah Beth Conroy, just in case you want to check or something."

"So you haven't seen Jesse this morning?"

"That's what I said. Guess you and Studley Do-right made a trip out here for nothing." She shot another glance at Dale. "There is such a thing as a telephone, you know. Look into it."

Grace took another step up the stairs as she fanned herself with her hand. "I've been out in this heat all morning. You think I could trouble you for a glass of ice water?"

Sookie stood there—arms still folded over her chest—and stared at Grace. Then she turned without a word and marched into the house.

She'd left the door open, so Grace took that as an invitation. She glanced back at Dale, inclined her head slightly toward the large garage that stood off to the side of the house, and then followed Sookie inside.

Grace stood in the spacious foyer for a

moment, letting her eyes adjust to the dimness. Off to the side of the front hall was a room Aggie had always called the parlor. Grace could detect a faint scent of fresh paint from that direction, and the hodge-podge of furniture crowded inside looked mostly brand new.

Up the curving staircase and third door down the hallway was the room where Grace had lost her virginity. Not a bad memory, but one she didn't particularly care to dwell on.

She followed the clip-clop of Sookie's boots down the hallway to the kitchen. There were changes here as well. Aggie's wallpaper and Coppertone appliances—ancient even back then—had been replaced with shiny stainless steel and sleek granite.

"Looks like Jesse is doing okay for himself," Grace said. "What's he up to these days?"

"Why don't you ask him for yourself when you see him?" Sookie filled a glass with crushed ice and water from the refrigerator door. "You said there'd been some trouble out at the canyon. What kind of trouble?"

"Some teenagers on four-wheelers found a body out there this morning."

The blond ponytail swayed wildly as

Sookie's head swung around to Grace, and her face darkened. "Who was it?"

Was that a note of fear that had crept into her voice?

"We haven't been able to make a positive ID yet."

"You don't have any idea who he is?"

"I never said the victim was male."

An *oh, damn* expression spread over Sookie's features. "Well, I just…I guess I assumed." She took a moment to find her composure. "If nobody knows who this person is, then he…she…must not be from around here. That's why you're asking about strangers, right?"

"Have you seen anybody like that around here?"

"Can't say as I have." She plunked the water glass down on the counter.

Grace took a couple of sips and returned the glass to the counter. "Do you know Cecelia Suarez? She's about your age, I think. Works for Colt McKinney."

"I know who she is, but we're not friends or anything. I see her at the Blue Moon sometimes. Why?"

"Have you ever heard her mention a brother?"

"You mean Sergio?" Revelation dawned then and Sookie's eyes widened as her hand crept to her chest. "Is he…?"

"Like I said, we haven't made an ID yet."

Sookie bit her lip. Two faint blotches of red stained her cheeks. "Look, I need to…I need to visit the little girl's room. I'll be right back."

She left the kitchen quickly, and Grace could hear the clatter of her boots hurrying down the hallway. A door closed and then the house fell silent.

And into that waiting quiet came a sound that sent a chill up Grace's spine.

A sound from her past.

From where she stood, she could see out the window. Just beyond the garage, an old wooden windmill pumped water into a metal tank.

The ginning sound of the blades took Grace back so thoroughly that when the wind puffed open the screen door on the back porch, she thought for a moment that someone had come inside. She whirled, but no one was there.

As she turned back, her gaze was drawn to the window again. Dale Walsh was just coming around the corner of the garage, and for some reason it was like Grace had unexpectedly caught sight of an old friend. She'd known him for less than a day and already she was getting used to having him around.

"What's so interesting out that window?"

Grace jumped at the sound of Sookie's voice behind her. Evidently, the woman could move about quietly in those boots when she had a mind to.

"Nothing." Grace turned. "I thought I heard someone on the back porch just now. Thought it might be Jesse."

"It's just the wind blowing the screen door. I must have left it unlatched when I came in earlier. You sure seem skittish for a cop."

You try getting shot at and see if you don't get a little skittish. "So, where were we? Oh, yeah, you were about to tell me how you know this Sergio fellow."

"I don't know him," Sookie rushed to assure her. "Never even met the guy. I've just heard Cecelia mention him a time or two."

"Is his last name Suarez?"

"I couldn't tell you."

"Has Cecelia ever mentioned where he lives?"

"Across the border somewhere. Nuevo Laredo, maybe."

Grace took another drink of water, then

walked over and put the glass in the sink. "That hit the spot," she said. "Thanks."

They went back out to the porch. The wind was hot and dry, and way out over the plains, Grace could see a dust devil spinning and dancing across the desert floor.

Dale leaned against the truck, arms folded, one foot crossed over the other as if he'd been there the whole time they'd been gone.

When they came down the steps, he gave a little wave and smiled, and Grace heard Sookie catch her breath.

Yeah, Grace thought. *I know.*

GRACE GAVE CAGE the lowdown on her conversation with Sookie Truesdale as they drove back to town. She was still unconvinced that Nance had been the shooter at the canyon, and since Cage hadn't found a smoking gun—literally or figuratively—in the garage or barn, she'd seen no reason to change her opinion.

But Cage wondered if her conviction had been dented by the fact that the guy hadn't been home, nor had his girlfriend been able, or at least willing, to provide him with an airtight alibi.

And now she knew the dead man's name was Sergio.

Cage could have told her that at the crime scene. He could have also informed her that the dead guy was directly connected to the murders in San Miguel, but instead he'd kept his mouth shut because he knew the moment he started talking, all hell was bound to break loose.

Cage sat gazing out the window at the passing brown scenery. The sun was like a burning flare overhead, the glare so extreme he had to squint behind his sunglasses. Little puffs of dust rolled across the desert, and he could feel the grit blowing in through the broken back window and drifting down the collar of his shirt.

Beside him, Grace scowled at the road. He turned to glance at her from time to time, but she seemed so lost in thought, he wasn't sure she was even aware of his presence. Her left hand was on the steering wheel and her right rested lightly on the seat beside her. He could see beads of blood on the tiny cuts, and a couple of her nails had been broken. She didn't seem to notice that, either.

He wondered where her thoughts had drifted to just now, and he wondered who wanted her dead.

Cage knew he couldn't let this go on for much longer. She had a right to know about the contents of that briefcase. But even if he could somehow manage to convince her that he had been nothing but an innocent by-stander to the shoot-out in San Miguel, she wouldn't be able to help him. She had no authority outside Cochise County, so when and if Cage was taken into custody, her hands would be tied.

Even so, he couldn't remain silent for much longer—not in good conscience. What kind of a man would he be if he risked her life just to save his own hide?

He turned back to the side window, letting his thoughts drift from one possible scenario to the next.

What if he could show her the briefcase without mentioning anything of what he'd witnessed in San Miguel?

That wouldn't work, though, because he knew how it would play out. First thing out of her mouth would be what happened to the real Dale Walsh. Then she'd want to know why, if Cage was so innocent, had he come to town with a stolen identity? Why hadn't he come clean from the get-go?

Unless he told her everything, his motivation didn't make much sense and would only serve to arouse her suspicions.

He still hoped, as he had the night before, that the person responsible for hiring the hit man would somehow make contact with him. Even though the transaction had likely been conducted anonymously, he—or she—would still be on the alert for a stranger riding into town. Cage had been there for less than twenty-four hours so some sort of communication was still a possibility. Unless the conspirator had decided to take matters into his own hands.

Maybe that same someone was the person who had fired at them from the canyon.

As they drove into town, Grace glanced at her watch. "It's past noon," she said. "You want to grab a bite to eat before we head back to the station?"

"Suits me."

She pulled into a space in front of the diner. "This place okay with you?"

"I'm not particular."

"The food is nothing to write home about, but it's convenient. I can run across the street to my room and get cleaned up." She glanced in the rearview mirror, saw the dried blood on the side of her face and grimaced. "I'd rather not be seen looking like this. People might think I'm not up to the job."

"Then again, they might think you're tough enough to handle whatever comes your way."

"Well, I guess we'll just have to see about that, won't we?"

They got out of the truck, and Cage watched as she strode across the street and disappeared inside Miss Nelda's. He went inside the diner, washed his hands and face in the bathroom, then took the same booth he'd had earlier at breakfast. A gray-haired waitress with a bad perm came over to take his order this time.

When she handed him a menu, he said, "There'll be two of us."

"Guess you'll need a moment then."

While he waited for Grace, Cage once again tried to figure out what he could do to affect the best outcome for both of them, but by the time she slid into the booth across from him, he was no closer to a solution than he had been the night before.

The only difference now was…he was getting to know her. And he liked her. Leaving the briefcase and skipping town just didn't seem like much of an option anymore.

They ordered club sandwiches and iced tea, and while they waited for their food,

Cage surreptitiously studied her. She'd changed from her black suit into a light gray one. The formal attire seemed more in keeping with her position at the TBI than as the sheriff of a rural county, but Cage suspected her conservative style was all part of the image she was trying so hard to cultivate. He wondered if she might be better served by lightening up a little, but he was hardly in any position to offer advice. Look at how his career had turned out.

"You sure look serious," she said.

"I've been sitting here thinking about the shooting."

"Have you come to any conclusions?"

"Only the obvious," he said. "Someone's out to get you."

"You were there, too," she reminded him.

"But that truck is clearly marked with the Sheriff's Department emblem on each side. I don't think it likely that I was the target. Besides, I haven't been in town long enough to make enemies."

"And you think I have?"

"You're the top dog," he said. "You've got enemies by the very nature of your job. Question is, do you have any idea who that enemy might be?"

She glanced out the window at the parking lot. "No. No idea."

"Have there been any other incidents?"

She paused. "You mean have I been fired upon before? Today was a first."

That wasn't what he meant and she knew it. She was being deliberately obtuse.

What are you hiding? Cage wondered.

She was still looking out the window, squinting slightly into the light. "You know, what you said is true. Enemies are inherent with a job like this. I think someone was sending the new sheriff a message today." She turned back to face him. "Whoever killed Sergio left that altar out there so that I would know they're here, in Cochise County. And that ambush—in the middle of the day, no less—was nothing but pure intimidation. They're testing me. And they're letting me know they're not afraid of the law."

"Could be," Cage said. "But from what I know about drug runners, they're not big on nuance. Their idea of subtlety is a bullet to the back of the head rather than a slit throat. I don't think taking a few pot shots is exactly their style."

"Normally, I would agree with you." Idly, Grace traced a drop of condensation down the side of her water glass. "The type of crime we get out here…it's different from anything I've ever seen before. The mindset of the criminal is different, too. But you're wrong about the subtlety. Even the most heinous murder you can imagine—has some sort of nuance. Some sort of message. They want us to be afraid. They want to use our fear to control us. But I'm not going to let that happen. I wouldn't have taken that oath if I hadn't been willing to die. And yes," she said with a wry smile. "I'm well aware of how melodramatic that sounds."

She really was something, Cage thought. He'd never met anyone with such a fierce sense of duty. It made him feel a little out of his league.

And when he thought of that briefcase, another of his mother's old sayings came to mind: *Son, you must be feeling lower than a snake's belly in a wagon rut for pulling a stunt like that.*

At that moment, he was feeling pretty low, all right. He was glad when the waitress brought over their food. It gave him a chance to change the subject because, God help him, he still didn't know what he was going to do about the briefcase.

"Tell me about Jesse Nance," he said, when they had both started to eat. "How did you two hook up?"

Grace dabbed her mouth with her napkin, then took a sip of tea. "We were together all through high school. On graduation night, a bunch of us went down to Tijuana. Jesse got the bright idea to propose, and Colt egged him on."

"Colt?"

"Colt McKinney. He was always the big instigator in our group. Anyway, the next thing I knew, I was waking up in the bridal suite at the Hotel Lafayette with the worst hangover of my life. Literally."

Cage grinned. "How did that go over with your family?"

"My grandmother nearly had a cow." She laughed, but there was a look of embarrassment in her eyes. "Looking back now, it seems hard to believe that I would do something that stupid and irresponsible. I like to think it was completely out of character for me."

"Or maybe you've just learned to subvert that side of your nature," Cage teased.

"I wish," she muttered.

"What did his folks think?"

"His dad was dead by then, but his mother always liked me. She used to say that I was good for Jesse, so she was happy about the elopement. I moved my stuff over to their place and settled in, but I knew right from the start it wasn't going to work. I hung around for most of the summer, and then when the fall semester started, I packed my bags, left for college and never looked back."

"And Jesse?"

She shrugged. "His mother was a lot more upset than he was. I think she kept hoping I'd get tired of school and come back home. Jesse didn't seem to care much one way or the other. He was always going to do what he wanted to do, wife or no wife. We got a quiet divorce, and most of the kids I knew at school never even knew I'd been married. I was kind of hoping people around here would have forgotten all about it."

"This is a small town. People have long memories and they like to talk. But you were what, eighteen? I doubt anybody's going to hold it against you."

"Probably not. But that whole ridiculous episode…" She shook her head in wonder.

"You think you're the only person who's ever made a stupid mistake?"

"No, of course not."

"You just don't like having any chinks in your armor, is that it?"

She met his gaze squarely. "No, I don't."

Cage sat back in his seat and studied her for a moment.

"What?" she asked with a frown.

"You're pretty hard on yourself, don't you think?"

"No." Her hand was on the table. She lifted it to examine the scratches, then dropped it to her lap. "If I don't have high expectations for myself, why should anyone else?"

She had a point, and Cage reckoned he could learn a thing or two from her about expectations.

"So this Colt McKinney that you mentioned…are he and Jesse still friends?"

"I guess so. They're probably not as close as they once were, though. You tend to outgrow people like Jesse Nance." She paused as the waitress came over to top off their tea glasses. "Why do you want to know about Colt and Jesse?"

"I saw them in here together this morning. They sat right behind my booth, and I couldn't help overhearing part of their conversation. Did you know that McKinney has made an offer on Jesse's ranch?"

Grace looked mildly surprised and not at all interested. "No, but it's really none of my business."

Cage couldn't let it go, though. Not quite yet. Something about that conversation still bothered him except he couldn't say why. "From what one of the waitresses told me, Jesse is pretty hard up for money."

"I'm not surprised. He never did know how to save a dime. But as far as being hard up…you couldn't tell that by all the new furniture and appliances I saw this morning at the house."

"Evidently, Sookie is a little on the high-maintenance side."

Grace rolled her eyes. "You think?"

"Here's the curious part of their conversation," Cage said. "They kept talking about some problem with the deed, and McKinney insisted that Jesse take care of it so he wouldn't have to get involved. Do you have any idea what kind of problem they might have been talking about?"

"Maybe something to do with his mother's will, I don't know. She died the same year I left for college. It happened pretty fast so she may not have had time to get her affairs in order." Grace was starting to look a little annoyed by the subject. "Anyway, like I said, it's none of my business. None of yours, either, is it? Why are you so interested in Jesse Nance?"

"You know why."

"Because you think he may have had something to do with the shooting. You know how I feel about that theory. I haven't see Jesse in years. It's a stretch to think he's carried a torch or a grudge or anything else since we split up. And as far as Colt buying the ranch, more power to him. I really don't care."

"Would you care if Colt McKinney wanted to buy your family's ranch?"

That got her attention. "He said that?"

"From what I overheard, he's expressed some interest. Jesse seemed to think it was a ploy to get him to lower his asking price."

"So that's where Lily got the idea to sell," Grace mused. "Colt must have approached her about it."

"Does she own the property outright?"

"My sisters and I own it together," Grace said. "We'd all have to agree to sell, but according to Lily, my older sister, Rachel, isn't going to be a problem."

"So does that leave you as the lone holdout?"

She shook her head. "I never said I wouldn't

sell. Lily just hit me with all of this yesterday. I've barely had time to think about it."

"Have you two ever talked about it? Is there some reason she may have gotten the impression you wouldn't want to sell?"

Grace's expression shut down. She glanced out over the diner. "Lily and I don't talk about much of anything these days." She paused as her gaze slid back to Cage. "You sure know how to pump someone for information, don't you?"

"It's all part of the job," he said, grinning.

"Some people are a little better at it than others," she murmured. "I'll have to remember that."

"I'm just taking your advice," Cage said. "Trying to get the lay of the land, so to speak."

"Right. So let's turn the tables for a while. Why don't you tell me something about yourself?"

"What do you want to know?"

She sat back against the booth and obviously tried to relax. "Well, did you always want to be a cop?"

"No, I always planned to play pro football. I was pretty good, too, back in the day. Until I blew out my knee."

"And that's when you decided to become

a cop?" There was a note of something—almost disapproval, he thought—in her voice.

"I had to be something," he said. "Law enforcement seemed as good a career as any."

She stared at him for a moment. "That surprises me."

"Why?"

"The way Charlie Dickerson talked about you, I had you pegged for the hardcore gung-ho type. You know, the kind who eat, breathe and sleep their badge."

"Well, we can't all be like you," he said.

"You think I'm hardcore?"

"You don't?"

She seemed to consider it for a moment, then shrugged it off. "I guess I have my days." She toyed with a pack of sweetener. "So have you ever been married?"

"Came close once, but it didn't work out. Being a cop is pretty tough on relationships. I guess you'd know that as well as anyone. What you said earlier about being willing to die—it's true," Cage said. "You have to have some acceptance of your own mortality to even do this job. The people who care about you aren't going to have that same acceptance. That's why the divorce rate among cops is so high."

"And suicide," she said.

"Well, now, that I don't get," he said. "I've seen my share of misery, but I still have a pretty high regard for my own skin."

"Right." She gave him a look. "That's why you ran out into the open like you did earlier. We need to talk about that. If you do come to work for my department, you need to remember that I call the shots. So, I need to ask you again if that's going to be a problem for you."

"It's not a problem," he said.

And it wouldn't be if he was really in the market for this job. Because Grace Steele had pretty much had him at hello.

Chapter Eleven

By the time Cage and Grace got back to the station, word of the shoot-out had spread like wildfire, and several of the deputies filed out of the building to have a look at the shot-up truck.

And unless Cage was mistaken, Grace's estimation seemed to go up with every whistle and "Aah" over the bullet holes in the metal and the shattered back glass.

But Lily, he noticed, was not among Grace's newfound admirers.

"We still need to have that sit-down interview," Grace said. "But I'm going to be swamped for the rest of the day. Any chance we could talk again tomorrow?"

"Sure, no problem. I've got things to keep me busy. I think I'll take your advice and do a little exploring on my own this afternoon."

As Cage pulled away from the station a

few minutes later, a small group of deputies were still crowded around Grace's truck, but she'd moved off to the side. Cage raised a hand in farewell, but she either didn't see him or didn't care to respond. She just stood there staring after him until he lost sight of her in the rearview mirror.

Cage put the top down as he drove out of town. The wind blowing against his face was exhilarating, and a part of him wanted to just keep going. But he only made it as far as the canyon. After pulling off the road, he climbed up to the top again and stood gazing around.

He could see for miles from that vantage, but there wasn't much to take in. Just the flat, featureless desert, populated by prairie dogs, lizards and the shadowy skeletons of head-high cholla cactus.

Taking care with his bad knee, Cage made his way to the other side of the canyon and followed along the rim until he found a trail that led down to the bottom. The path was rugged, but he figured it would accommodate a four-wheeler with an experienced driver at the helm.

Cage was wearing shades, but the sun was so bright, he had to shield his eyes as he gazed off across the plains. He could see the silhouette of the Nance ranch house to the east, but in such an empty landscape, distance was hard to judge.

If Nance had been the shooter, he could have made it down the canyon, taken cover somewhere along the base until Cage and Grace left, then hightailed it across the desert in plenty of time to ditch the four-wheeler and hide out before they showed up on his doorstep. Of course, that would mean he'd somehow known that Grace would be at the crime scene that morning.

She didn't think Jesse was responsible for the shooting, but Cage wasn't so convinced. The proximity of his ranch and his and Grace's history made him at least a person of interest in Cage's book.

And there was still something about that overheard conversation at the diner that morning that niggled at Cage.

Once he made his way down the canyon, he climbed into the Caddy and drove back into town. He found a parking spot near the courthouse, which was one of those great old buildings with a domed roof and Victorian-style woodwork. Silhouetted against the blue sky and a backdrop of distant mountains, the courthouse seemed to embody the spirit of West Texas, complete with a broken statue of Justice on top of the dome.

Cage located the county clerk's office, but there was no one behind the counter. However, through the open door of one of the offices, he could see a young man reared back in a chair, feet propped on the desk, absorbed in a *Soldier of Fortune* magazine.

When Cage knocked on the counter, the sound startled the poor guy so badly, he almost tumbled out of his chair. Scrambling to his feet, he shoved the magazine in a drawer and straightened his glasses as he came through the door.

"Can I help you?"

He looked to be in his late twenties, a buttoned-up type in khaki pants and loafers. Not exactly the target demographic for *Soldier of Fortune,* Cage thought, but then computer nerds were the ones who went so insane for all those online war games.

"I'm interested in a piece of property in Cochise County, and I need to take a look at the deed. Can you help me do that?" Cage asked him.

The clerk took some time to adjust his glasses. "If the deed has been recorded, I can locate it for you. But I'll need a physical description of the property or a tax parcel number."

"Well, I don't have either of those things," Cage said. "I can give you a name. I already know who owns the property, but I've been made aware of a possible problem with the deed. That's why I want to take a look and see what I'm getting into."

"What's the name?"

"Jesse Nance."

The man gave him a curious look before he disappeared back into one of the offices.

When he came back out several minutes later, he put some papers on the counter and motioned Cage over. "I made copies of the deed and all the recent transfers that I thought you might be interested in."

Cage stared down at the first document. "Okay, what am I looking at?"

"This is a copy of the deed that was issued to Harold and Agatha Nance. When Harold died—" he shuffled the papers "—his wife had to fill out this transfer in order to remove his name from the deed."

"And this one?" Cage pointed to the third paper.

"This is the last deed on record. It transfers

the property to Jesse Nance and his wife, Grace Steele Nance."

Cage stared at Grace's name on the paper. Adrenaline kicked his blood pressure up a notch. "Let me get this straight. The name Grace Steele Nance is on the latest copy of the deed."

"The last one on record," the clerk said. "Deeds aren't always recorded. There could be another copy that we don't know about. But in order for it to be legal, Jesse Nance would have needed Grace Steele Nance's signature on a transfer to remove her name."

"Let's say this is the latest deed," Cage said. "What if Jesse Nance wanted to sell the property?"

"Same thing. He'd need her signature."

"So in essence, Grace owns half this property."

"I guess that would be for a court to decide."

"How much is the property worth?"

"You can go to the tax assessor's office to find out the latest appraisal. Of course, what a property is appraised at, and what it's worth to a particular buyer are two different things."

Cage picked up the papers. "Can I keep these copies?"

"Sure. Everything here is a matter of public record."

Cage nodded. "Thanks. You've been a big help...I didn't catch your name."

"Brennan. Ethan Brennan."

"Thanks, Ethan."

"No problem. Listen, I probably shouldn't mention this..." His gaze shot to the door as if to make sure no one was listening. "You're not the first person who's been in here looking at that deed. Someone else is interested in that property, and unless you've got deep pockets—"

"Colt McKinney, right?"

One brow lifted in surprise. "You already know about him, then."

"I know he's interested in this property, and I know he has deep pockets."

"Not just deep pockets," Ethan said. "He has a way of getting whatever he wants, and sometimes money has nothing to do with it. If you plan to make an offer on Nance's ranch...just watch your back, is all I'm saying."

"I appreciate the heads-up," Cage said. "You wouldn't have any idea what his plans are for this place, would you?"

"No more than I know what your plans are for it," he said. "It's pretty remote and the terrain is rugged out there. But I guess you already know that. You probably also know that only a few hundred feet separate the edge of Nance's property from Mexico. If someone needed easy access to the border and plenty of places to hide out..." He trailed off on a shrug, but his eyes behind his glasses took on a sly glint that made Cage wonder how often people underestimated the guy.

Before Cage was out the door, Ethan had gone back to his magazine.

Outside, Cage stood for a moment glancing around the town square. Across the street was an old-fashioned movie theater with *Rialto* spelled out in green, purple and pink neon. The lights were turned off and the ticket window boarded up, the victim, no doubt, of a new multiplex somewhere in town. The square was deserted and quiet, which was why the black SUV that idled at the corner caught his eye.

It was a late model and expensive, with windows tinted so darkly, Cage couldn't see a soul inside. But it wasn't hard to imagine a pair of cold, cold eyes staring back at him.

COLT MCKINNEY'S RANCH was a far cry from Jesse's place. The sprawling hacienda-style home with its stucco walls and red-tile roof gleamed like a jewel in the hot afternoon sunlight as Grace sailed down the paved drive.

Rows of metal wind turbines pumped the precious life blood of West Texas onto an acre of green lawn dotted with flower beds and fruit trees, making it an oasis of bright colors and thick, cool shade.

Grace pulled around the circular drive and parked in front of the house. Cecelia Suarez answered the door. She had a youthful face, but her dark eyes seemed to reflect an old soul, the kind that came with too much hard experience at too tender an age. She was dressed in a turquoise smock embroidered with red and yellow flowers, and her thick black hair was held back from her face with a red plastic headband, showcasing those long-suffering eyes and high cheekbones that hinted at an Indian ancestry.

"Sheriff Steele," she said in surprise. Her English was nearly perfect, with just the barest trace of an accent. "Mr. McKinney isn't here. Was he expecting you?"

"I came to see you, Cecelia. May I come in?"

"Yes, of course," she said, her expression puzzled as she stepped back for Grace to enter.

The house was cool and breezy inside and the rotation of the ceiling fans stirred Cecelia's hair as she led Grace back toward the kitchen, her brown sandals slapping softly against the slate floor.

Grace followed her down the wide hallway, past arched doorways and long windows through which she glimpsed lush courtyards and shady loggias.

The house was spotless, Grace noticed. Whatever Colt paid Cecelia, he was certainly getting his money's worth. As if reading her mind, Cecelia glanced over her shoulder, her earlier bewilderment now turning to worry.

The kitchen was at the back of the house, a huge, airy room filled with the smell of fresh-baked bread. Cecelia motioned to one of the leather stools at the handcrafted bar. "I just made some lemonade. Would you like a glass?"

"That sounds nice," Grace said as she perched on the nearest stool. When the sweating glass was before her, she took a sip and smiled appreciatively. "Delicious."

Cecelia stood nervously on the other side of the counter, her arms stiffly at her side. "What did you want to see me about? I haven't done anything wrong, have I?"

"No, of course not. I need to ask you some questions about your brother."

"Sergio?" Now she looked really distressed. "Is he in some sort of trouble?"

"I'm sorry to have to tell you this…" Oh, how Grace hated this part of her job. "A body was found near Red Rock Canyon this morning. One of the deputies thinks the victim may be your brother."

"Mi Dios." She quickly crossed herself.

"We'll need you to come down to the morgue later to identify the body."

She closed her eyes and nodded. "When?"

"I can drive you there now if you want. Or I can send a car to pick you up later."

"That's okay. I have my own car."

"This is not something you want to do alone," Grace said. "Call me when you're ready and I'll meet you over there."

The young woman nodded. Her eyes were dry, but her knuckles had whitened where she gripped the edge of the bar.

"When was the last time you saw your brother?" Grace asked.

"Sergio is my half brother. We have different fathers."

"What's his last name?"

"Garcia Gonzalez."

Grace took out her notebook and jotted the information down.

"I saw him two weeks ago," Cecelia said. "But only briefly. He wasn't in town for long."

"Have you talked to him since then?"

She shook her head sadly. "We don't keep in touch. My mother brought me back to America when I was little, and Sergio stayed with his father. So we aren't close. And some of the things he does…his *compadres*…" She used the term as a slang. *"Diablos,"* she said with a shudder.

"Has your brother ever been involved in drug smuggling? Does he work for one of the cartels?"

"I don't know. I never asked. But from the company he keeps…" She lifted a shoulder in resignation.

"Is there anyone else in this area that Sergio might have come to see?"

Something flickered in the woman's eyes before she glanced away. "No one that I know."

"Where does your brother live?"

"Nuevo Laredo, last I heard."

"Is there anyone that we should get in touch with?"

Cecelia shook her head. "Our parents are dead. I'm the only family he has left." She looked down at her hands, hiding whatever emotion that might have been revealed in her eyes.

"When you're ready to go to the morgue, give me a call." Grace handed her a card.

Cecelia slipped the card into her pocket without a glance.

"And if there's anything I can do—"

"Grace?"

At the sound of the male voice behind her, she turned to see Colt standing in the doorway. He looked as handsome and elegant as ever, even with his sleeves rolled up and his white shirt damp from perspiration. His suit coat was slung over his shoulder, and as he came into the room, he removed his sunglasses, his gaze going from Grace to Cecelia and back again.

"What are you doing out here?" he asked, and then before she could answer, he said, "I hope you can stay for lunch. I'm sure Cecelia can whip us up an omelet or a salad or something."

"Thanks, but I can't stay," Grace said. "I have to get back to the station."

Cecelia, head still bowed, said, "Will you excuse me?" and hurried from the room.

Colt glanced after her. "What's going on? She looked upset."

"A body was found this morning near Red Rock Canyon. We think the victim may be her brother, Sergio."

"Well, I can't say that would surprise me," Colt said. "That guy had bad news written all over him."

"You knew him?"

"I saw him in town with Cecelia on a couple of occasions. Luckily, he never came out here to see her. Not that I knew of anyway. I don't need his kind of problem," he said with an unfamiliar edge to his tone. Normally, his voice was as smooth as liquid.

"I asked Cecelia if she thought he might be connected to one of the cartels. What do you think?"

"Do the math, Grace. What is the percentage of murders along the border that are drug related?"

She nodded. "Did you ever see him with anyone else?"

"No. I don't think he came around these parts too often. He and Cecelia didn't get along."

"Didn't get along or weren't close?"

He shrugged.

"So why was he here last night?" Grace mused.

"I'm sure you'll figure it out," Colt said.

"You're a heck of a cop. That's why we brought you down here." He hung his coat on the back of one of the stools. "You sure you don't want to stay for lunch?"

"I've already had lunch, and besides, I have to get back." She rose to leave. "Oh, just one other thing…did you approach Lily about buying the ranch?"

He scrubbed a hand across his face. "She told you about that, huh?"

"Why didn't you tell me?"

"For one thing, I didn't approach her. Lily came to me. She wanted to know if I'd be interested in the property and I told her I might be if the price was right. And secondly, I didn't mention it to you because I didn't think it was my place to. I figured if Lily wanted you to know about that conversation, she'd tell you herself."

"So are you interested in buying it?" Grace asked.

He smiled. "Like I said, if the price is right."

"But aren't you buying Jesse's ranch?"

Colt looked surprised and none too pleased that she knew about that. "Where did you hear that?"

"Is it a secret?"

"Nothing around here is a secret," he said

dryly. "I've made him an offer, but we haven't signed the agreement yet."

"What's the holdup?"

"Gee, Grace, since when did you become so interested in my business affairs? There's nothing illegal about buying a piece of property, is there?"

"I guess I'm just curious why you want so much land when you already own half the county."

"I've got plans for that place." He poured himself a glass of lemonade from the pitcher Cecelia had left on the bar. "You try this?" he asked as he lifted the glass to his lips. "I don't know what she puts in here, but if she could bottle this damn stuff, she'd make a fortune. Best lemonade I ever had."

"What kind of plans?" Grace pressed.

Carefully, he set the glass aside. "Did you know that the Nance Ranch and the Steele Ranch both used to belong to the McKinneys? I got the idea some time back that I'd like to get the ranch back to the way it was in my grandfather's time. Back in its heyday. But I'm not going to put cattle out there on the Nance place," he said. "I want to use it to rescue wild horses."

Grace stared at him in surprise. She had

always liked Colt and thought him basically a good guy. But he'd never struck her as the philanthropic type. "That certainly sounds like a noble cause," she said. And come to think of it, Grace could see how those plans would appeal to Lily. It would be a great leverage for Colt. "Did you talk to my sister about these lofty plans of yours?"

"You sound a little skeptical," he said. "But don't think this is just some ploy to lure Lily into selling. I'm serious about this. You know all those wild horses the Bureau of Land Management recently rescued? Well, their plan now is to euthanize them or else sell them to the highest bidder without restriction, which means anyone can adopt a horse for any purpose they want. And all because of a budget snafu. So all those magnificent creatures are going to be slaughtered wholesale if someone doesn't step in. I'm just trying to do my part to preserve some of our heritage, that's all."

"Wow," Grace said. "I can see you're passionate about this."

"Deeply. I'd love to tell you more about it when you've got the time." His phone rang and he glanced at the display. "Sorry. I have to take this."

"Go ahead," Grace said. "I need to get back to the station anyway. I'll let myself out."

She went out the rear door and as she followed the drive around to the front, she noticed a four-wheeler off to the side of the garage. Nothing unusual about that. It was like she told Dale. Every rancher she knew used four-wheelers these days. Colt had a whole fleet, along with Jeeps and the helicopter he used for roundup.

Grace shot a glance toward the house, then went over to have a closer look. The ATV was covered in dust and as she squatted beside it, she noticed what looked to be a bullet nick in the rear fender.

Dusting her hands off as she rose, she glanced back over her shoulder. Someone stood at the kitchen window, but Grace caught only a quick glimpse before the silhouette moved back out of her sight.

Chapter Twelve

When Lily Steele slid onto the bar stool next to Cage's that night at the Blue Moon, he almost didn't recognize her. He did a double take and she laughed. "I love getting that response."

"I'll just bet you do." Cage couldn't get over the change. Her long hair hung to her waist, as black and glossy as India ink, and the pale blue sundress she wore showed off well-toned arms and sleek, suntanned legs.

Some ol' boy wasn't going to know what hit him tonight, Cage thought in amusement.

But despite the soft, womanly touches, he detected a hint of the old Lily in the brittle gleam of her gray eyes, in the mocking way she smiled at his reaction.

"Buy me a drink?"

He motioned for the bartender. When the frosty mugs of beer were placed before them, Lily picked hers up and took a long, thirsty swallow.

Cage used the opportunity to glance around. For a Thursday night, the place was jumping. The dance floor off to his right was already crowded, and over the blare of music he could hear hoots and hollers from the other end where a couple of pool tables had been placed. The rough-hewn walls were decorated with Texas flags, license plates and neon Lone Star beer signs.

"So, I heard what happened out at Red Rock Canyon this morning," Lily said. She swayed on the stool as she leaned toward him, making Cage wonder how much she'd already had to drink. "Tell me something, Walsh. Why is it my sister has all the fun around here?"

He quirked a brow. "You call a shoot-out fun?"

"Beats pushing a pencil all day."

Her cavalier tone made him a little angry, especially when he thought of all those months he'd spent in rehab. "You only think that because you've never been shot at before."

"Maybe I have, maybe I haven't. But I know how to handle a gun." Her smile taunted him. "I'll wager you do, too."

"Well, I wouldn't be much of a cop if I didn't, now would I?"

"Yeah, but there are guns and then there are guns," she said, tossing those glossy tresses over one shoulder. "Tell me something else, Mr. Dale Walsh. What does someone like you see in my sister?"

"I'm sorry?"

"Oh, come on." She gave him an accusing look as she propped an elbow on the bar. "I've seen the way you look at her."

"You've only met me once before tonight," he reminded her. "So, there's that. And as for your sister, I don't know what you think you saw, but I have nothing but the utmost respect for her."

"Blah…blah…blah. This is telling me one thing…" Lily mimicked his lip movement with her fingers. "But your eyes are saying something else. You like her."

"I like a lot of people. I even like you. Though you don't make it easy," he said ruefully.

She shrugged. "At least with me, what you see is what you get."

"Meaning?"

She leaned in, so close he could smell the beer on her breath and the perfume emanating from her creamy skin. "You say you have the utmost respect for my sister. What would you say if I told you she didn't exactly get this job on her own merit?"

"After seeing her in action? I'd say I find that hard to believe."

She scowled at his answer. "Oh, boy, does she have you buffaloed. Grace is our new sheriff for one reason and one reason only— Colt McKinney bullied the other commissioners into agreeing to hire her because he wanted her back in Jericho Pass."

"And why's that?"

"Because he's had the hots for her since high school. If I were you," Lily said with a sly smile, "I'd watch my back."

That made twice he'd received the same warning regarding Colt McKinney. Cage was beginning to think it might be time to meet this guy. "I'll take that under advisement," he said.

She pointed her finger like a gun and gave him a wink. "You do that." She polished off her beer and slid the glass aside. "Did you really mean what you said? You like me?"

"You're okay," Cage said with a grin.

"Then come dance with me."

"How do you know I can dance?"

"Just call it a hunch," she said as she

hopped off the stool and grabbed his hand. "I have a feeling you can *dance* like there's no tomorrow."

"BUY YOU A DRINK?" Colt leaned an arm against the bar.

"One more," Grace said. "But that's my limit."

"Whatever you say."

He motioned to the bartender, and Grace was soon sipping a fresh beer. "What brings you to the Blue Moon?" she asked. "This doesn't exactly seem like your kind of hangout."

He grinned down at her. "Now, why would you say that? I like beer and pool as much as the next guy. And a little slumming now and then is good for a man's soul. I also happen to like the scenery," he said, giving her a long appraisal.

Grace rolled her eyes. "Oh, brother. How many of those have you had tonight?"

"I'm stone-cold sober," he said. "And you are looking good, Grace. Better than you did in high school, and that's saying something. Some women are like that…they just keep getting better and better."

She leaned back and stared at him. "What has gotten into you tonight?"

"I'm in a good mood," he said. "Anything wrong with that?"

"No, of course not." She sipped her beer and glanced around. Her gaze lit on her sister and—wait—was that Dale Walsh that Lily was dancing with? It *was* Dale Walsh.

For a moment, Grace couldn't tear her gaze away. They were dancing to a song with a beat that would have been impossible for her to keep time to, but they had no trouble at all. Lily looked so…young and uninhibited, like she was having the time of her life. She was laughing with abandon as she swung her head back and forth, making her long hair go crazy. Grace hadn't seen her sister laugh like that in a very long time.

She felt a twinge of—not jealousy, surely, but—yes, maybe it was jealousy. Grace had never been able to let herself go like that. She was always too afraid she might look silly, and too worried about how she would come across to other people.

As she watched, Lily moved in closer and Dale put his hand on her waist. The way he stared down at her sister, the way he *moved*…

The twinge of jealousy turned into a tight little curl of longing in the pit of Grace's stomach. She wanted Dale Walsh to put his hand on her waist like that. She wanted him to look at her the way he was smiling down at Lily. It was stupid and reckless and it made no sense because Grace had only known him for a day. But there it was. She wanted Dale Walsh.

Not that she would do anything about it, of course. She had too much at stake, and God, what a nightmare that would be if he did come to work for the department.

Beside her, Colt said, "Is that Lily? Whoa, she looks *hot...*"

"Watch it," Grace warned. "She's still my little sister."

"She's also gorgeous," Colt said, looking thoroughly taken aback. "How did I miss that?" He scowled suddenly as he continued to watch her. "Who's she dancing with?"

"That's Dale Walsh."

He swung around in amazement. "Dale Walsh? Are you sure?"

Grace laughed. "I spent most of the day with him today, so yeah, I'm pretty sure."

"But I thought—"

"That he'd be older? Me, too. He's not exactly what I expected, either."

Colt downed his drink and motioned to the bartender for another. "So what's the deal with him and Lily?"

"I suppose she's just trying to be friendly."

"Looks a little more than that to me," Colt muttered. "Do you see the way she keeps glancing over here? I think she's trying to get your goat, Grace. Now, why would she think her dancing with the new guy would annoy you?"

"I have no idea what Lily thinks about anything," Grace said. "I've given up trying to understand her."

"You really don't know what her problem is with you, do you?" Colt turned away from the dance floor and propped an arm on the bar.

"Are you saying you do?"

"Don't you remember the way she used to follow us around all the time? Especially our whole senior year. We couldn't go anywhere that she didn't turn up."

Grace shrugged. "So? That's what little sisters do."

"Yeah, but she wasn't doing it to annoy you or because she wanted to be cool or anything like that. She was trying to get Jesse's attention."

"What?"

"Grace, your sister was crazy about Jesse Nance."

"*No,*" Grace scoffed. "She was just a kid."

"She was fourteen. Plenty old enough to be madly in love, or at least think she was. She got her heart broken when you married Jesse."

"But…" Grace glanced helplessly at the dance floor. "I didn't know she had a crush on Jesse. She never said anything. And anyway, that was so long ago. She can't possibly still be upset about that."

"It wasn't just that. You were always the golden girl around here. Everyone expected great things from you."

"I'm the one who ran off and got married at eighteen," Grace reminded him. She tucked her hair behind one ear, trying not to compare her conservative bob to her sister's glorious tresses. She'd once had hair like Lily's, but she'd cut it all off because she thought it unprofessional. Long hair wasn't in keeping with the image she wanted to project. "Hardly a golden girl," she muttered.

"But that didn't stop you, did it? You had things you wanted to do so you went off and did them without a backward glance, and Lily stayed here. When your grandmother's health started failing, she was the only one left to take care of her. She didn't get to start a new life the way you and Rachel did. But she made the most of what was available to her, and then you waltzed back into town when things didn't go so great in Austin, and took the job she's worked her whole adult life for."

"But you're the one who offered me that job," Grace said. "You told me Lily was too young and inexperienced to even be considered."

"And she is. But she doesn't see it that way."

Grace sighed. "I should never have come back here."

"Of course you should," Colt said. "We need you and this is your home. This is where you belong. And if I have my way, you won't be leaving anytime soon."

Grace looked over at him. Something in his voice—

No, she'd imagined that wistful note, that faint trace of longing.

She glanced away quickly, not wanting to see something in his eyes that might ruin their friendship.

As if sensing her awkwardness, he straightened. "I think I see an open pool table," he said. "You up for a little Eight-ball?"

"I think I'll shove off. I'm pretty beat." Grace wasn't even sure why she'd come here tonight. This was her sister's world, after all, and Grace felt like an interloper. That was probably how Lily saw her, too.

After Colt left, Grace saw a familiar face at the end of the bar. It was Ethan Brennan. She almost didn't recognize him without his glasses. He was dressed all in black with a leather cord around his neck.

He noticed her then and gave a sheepish wave, as if embarrassed to be seen there. About that time, a blonde came up behind him and put her hands over his eyes. When he reached up and pulled them away, she giggled and sat down at the bar beside him.

Grace had no trouble at all recognizing Sookie Truesdale. She had on something low cut and sexy, and she kept leaning toward Ethan as if to make sure he got an eyeful.

"Can I buy you a drink?"

Startled by Dale's voice in her ear, Grace spun on the stool, grateful she'd managed not to fall off.

"I've already had two," she said. "That's my limit. The last thing I want is to wake up with another Tijuana hangover. Not that you would ever...we would ever..."

"I get your drift." He motioned for the bartender. "What are you doing here?" he said. "This doesn't exactly seem like your kind of place."

"I was just telling Colt McKinney the same thing."

"He's here?" Dale straightened, his gaze sweeping over the crowd.

"He's in the back playing pool," Grace said. "Why?"

Dale shrugged. "I've heard a lot about him since I hit town. Just wondered what the hype was all about."

"He has his moments, just like everyone else," Grace said. "And speaking of moments…I saw you dancing with Lily earlier. Did you two come here together?"

Dale gave her a little smile. "Would it bother you if we did?"

"Why would it bother me? Your personal life is your own business. I was just admiring the way you danced together, that's all."

He was still smiling at her in a funny little way that made her insides tingle. "Would you like to dance?"

"Me? Nooo. I've got two left feet. I'm a terrible dancer."

"There are no bad dancers," he said. "Just bad partners."

"I don't think that's true."

"It is," he said. "Just think about it."

"Well, maybe I'll test out your theory next time," she said as she slid off the stool. "Right now, I'm headed home."

"Mind if I walk you out?" His expression sobered. "There's something I need to talk to you about."

She shrugged. "Sure."

Outside, the night was still warm, but the breeze that swept in from the desert was cool. The music followed them out, and from somewhere in the parking lot came the sound of raucous laughter. For some reason, Grace was reminded of Sookie Truesdale, and she wondered again about the woman's overt flirtation with Ethan Brennan. Where was Jesse while all this was going on?

"Where's your truck?" Dale asked.

"I walked over."

He glanced down at her in the dark. "I'm not so sure that's a smart thing to do, considering what happened this morning."

"It's just a few blocks," Grace said.

"Just a few blocks is plenty of time to be shot at or nabbed."

"Well, that's a cheery little thought, but your point is taken. I'll be more careful from now on."

"Promise?"

She started to laugh, but his voice sounded dead serious. "Yeah. I promise." His intensity unsettled her a bit. "So, what did you want to talk to me about?"

He glanced around. The parking lot was almost as crowded as the dance floor, with people milling about smoking and laughing, a few couples necking. "I'd rather not talk here," he said. "I can give you a lift home. My car is right over there."

Grace glanced over at the old Caddy, the gleaming paint highlighting the classic lines. "That car suits you," she was surprised to hear herself say.

"Because it's old and tacky?" he teased.

"Because it has style," she said. "It may not be to everyone's taste, but there's nothing ordinary about it."

"Well, thanks…I guess. So how about a ride?"

They were standing next to the car by this time, and Grace ran her hand over the tailfin. "These things make it look like it could fly."

"It can," he said. "Hop in and I'll show you."

THE NEXT THING GRACE KNEW, they were sailing out through the desert. The top was down, and with the wind in her hair and a blanket of stars overhead, it did feel a little like flying.

She pointed to a cutoff just ahead. "That's the road to Willow Springs. The ghost town I told you about. It's really not much more than a track," she said. "You almost need an ATV to get there nowadays. The bridge over the arroyo is in pretty bad shape so I'm not even sure I'd want to risk it on a four-wheeler." When Cage pulled off the highway and onto the trail, she said in alarm, "You're not going to try it in this car, I hope."

He stopped, put the car in Park and killed the engine.

"What are you doing?" she asked, not the least bit frightened but more nervous than she would have thought possible.

"I told you, I need to talk to you about something. Out here, where there aren't any prying eyes or big ears. Just the coyotes and the stars." He tilted his head back and watched a meteorite shoot across the sky. And then another and another. "Whoa. I don't think I've ever seen anything like that."

"You can see meteor showers all the time out here." She laid her head back against the seat and gazed upward. "This sky was what

I missed most when I moved to San Antonio. After a while, you get used to not seeing stars. Then you come back out here and you're reminded on a night like this, with a ghost town in front of you and the desert behind you and all those stars twinkling overhead, that West Texas is just about the most romantic place on earth."

She turned her head on the seat and looked at him in the dark. "Don't laugh at me," she warned.

He turned his head, too, and she could feel his gaze on her in the dark. "I'm not laughing, Grace."

She perceived his head moving closer, and Grace caught her breath. "That's a bad idea," she said.

"Blame it on the stars. Blame it on West Texas." He reached out and curved his fingers around her neck, pulling her toward him.

"We can't do this."

"I know we can't. But I've been thinking about it all night. You don't have any idea just how truly gorgeous you are. I've wanted to kiss you ever since I walked into your office and saw you behind that desk. Even before then."

"That's not possible. You never saw me

before then. And if you tell me you saw me in your dreams, I'll never be able to take you seriously again."

He grinned, but something dark glinted in his eyes. "Are you sure this is such a bad idea? Just one kiss?"

"Put it this way. If you kiss me, you'll be out of a job. I won't be able to hire you."

"Might be worth it," he murmured.

"You're just letting your hormones talk," she said. "Maybe we should drive back to town before they say something you and I will both regret."

"Okay, you're right. No romance tonight." He flopped back against his seat and gazed up at the sky. "But I still need to talk to you about something that, trust me, will be a real mood killer."

"I'm listening." Grace was amazed at how normal her voice sounded when her insides were such a mess. What was she doing out here anyway with a man she hardly knew? What in the world had possessed her to consider even for a moment—to still be considering—what the harm would be in just one kiss?

She knew the answer to that.

Because a kiss was never just a kiss.

There would be touching and more

kissing, kissing and more touching, and the moment would come, sooner or later, when she'd have to decide if she wanted to have sex more than she wanted a deputy.

It was ridiculous to even contemplate such a choice. She was a grown woman, a professional, not some eighteen-year-old girl who had let her libido and a few tequila shots get the better of her.

"Grace? Are you listening to me?"

She roused herself. "I'm sorry. What did you say?"

He was holding some papers in his hand. "Did you know that your name is on the deed to Jesse Nance's ranch?"

It took a moment for the words to penetrate her addled brain, and then Grace scoffed at him. "No, it isn't. Who told you that?"

"I've got the evidence right here." He held up the papers. "This is a copy of the deed. You can see for yourself."

He reached over and fished a flashlight out of the glove box, then angled the beam over the paper so that Grace could skim it. Sure enough, there was her name. Grace Steele Nance.

She glanced up. "There must be some mistake."

"There's no mistake," Cage said. "Unless

you signed a transfer that would have allowed him to take your name off the deed."

"I signed divorce papers," Grace said. "There was nothing about a deed."

"You said his mother was happy about the marriage. She must have signed the deed over without telling either one of you about it. Jesse probably didn't know about it himself until he wanted to sell the ranch. And then he couldn't without your signature."

"So, why hasn't he asked me to sign something?"

"Because legally half of that land is yours. And depending on what McKinney is offering, half could be a lot. You see what this means, don't you?"

Grace looked over at him. "It doesn't prove anything. We have to be careful here with any accusations."

"You're right," Cage said. "It doesn't prove anything. But you have to admit, it does give your ex-husband a pretty strong motive for murder."

Chapter Thirteen

When Cage pulled up in front of Miss Nelda's a little while later, Grace said, "Why don't I go inside and you use the outside stairs to the balcony. I don't see the point of giving the sisters something to speculate about."

"Fine by me."

She opened the door and climbed out, then turned back. "I'm going to hang on to this if you don't mind." She held up the copy of the deed.

"It's yours," Cage said. He watched her until she was inside the house, and then he put the top up, got out and locked the doors. A vehicle turned the corner behind him, and as Cage glanced over his shoulder, he heard the motor gun as the driver accelerated.

Quickly, he stepped into the shadows at the corner of the house and watched as the car approached. It was a silver SUV with a techno beat blasting from the open windows.

A beer bottle exploded on the street and then the vehicle shot forward, careened around the next corner and disappeared.

Just a bunch of kids, Cage thought, with a driver who obviously had no business being behind the wheel. He watched for a moment to see if they came back, and as he turned toward the steps, a hand fell on his shoulder.

Cage whirled and almost whacked the person behind him until he realized in the nick of time that it was Miss Nelda. She jumped back, her hand at her heart.

"Oh, dear, you scared me half to death!"

"Likewise," Cage said. "I didn't hear you come up behind me."

Now that she had her poise back, she gave him a sly smile. "Using the side stairs? It's a good thing Billy Don came over and fixed that light for Sister and me so now you'll be able to see where you're going." She glanced at the street where his car was pulled to the curb. "Oh, how that car takes me back. My fiancé had one just like it in fire-engine red." She clasped her hands together and held them to her heart. "It was the most beautiful thing I ever saw, and he looked so dashing behind the wheel. Just like Robert Taylor in *Magnificent Obsession.* Did you ever see that movie, dear? It's about a man who falls madly in love with a woman whose life he feels responsible for, but he conceals his identity from her, making it impossible for them to ever be together."

"Sounds like a chick flick," Cage said, although he was starting to wonder about Miss Nelda. She either had uncanny instincts or she'd been doing some heavy-duty snooping. He had a feeling it was a little of both.

"It was wonderfully romantic," she said. "And everything turned out all right in the end because when he operated on her to remove a brain tumor, he also restored her sight, which she'd been told was gone forever. So, you see? Things have a way of working out for the best, especially when you do the right thing."

Uh, yeah, in movies, Cage thought. Real life was a different matter.

"Well, I won't keep you," she said. "I imagine you're anxious to get to bed." Her gaze traveled up the stairs to the balcony where a light in Grace's room had just come on. "Good night, dear."

"Good night, Miss Nelda."

Cage went up the stairs and let himself into his room. He took the briefcase from its hiding place, set it on the bed and popped the latches. Everything was still inside, just the way he'd left it—the guns, the cash, the envelope containing Grace's photo.

He took the picture out and studied it. His gaze was drawn to her lips, so full and ripe and delectable. He'd wanted to kiss her earlier. Badly. Still did. But first he had to make things right with her. Because he realized now, after spotting the SUV at the courthouse earlier that day and just now with the scare in front of the house, that it was very possible he'd have to leave town on a moment's notice. And there was no way he could skip out without telling her—without proving to her—the nature of the danger she faced.

There was a right way to do this. If he was careful, he and Grace might both come out of this alive.

Snapping the latches closed, he picked up the briefcase, went out the balcony door and strode down to her room.

WHEN GRACE HEARD the soft knock at the balcony door, she knew exactly who was out there. And she did not want to let him in. She told herself if she just ignored him, he'd finally get the message and go away.

But in spite of her best judgment, she found herself opening the door, one hand on her hip as she gazed up at him.

"What?"

He was taken aback by her abrupt tone. "I just want to talk to you."

"It's late, and we've done a lot of talking already tonight." Too much, maybe. "Can't this wait until morning?"

"No. I really need to get this off my chest tonight."

Grace noticed the briefcase then, and she said, "What's in there?"

"That's what I want to talk to you about. It can't wait any longer."

She stood back. "Okay. But make it quick. And please keep your voice down. I can just imagine what the sisters would think if they heard you in here. It would be all over town by morning."

He stepped inside and closed the door behind him.

He looks nervous, Grace thought. Nervous and wired.

Placing the briefcase on the table, he turned. "Before I start, I just want to say that I did what I thought was right at the time and I hope you won't judge me too harshly."

"Well, that sounds ominous."

"Just…promise you'll hear me out and keep an open mind. Here." He pulled out a chair from the table. "Maybe you better sit down for this."

"I'm fine," she said, although she was starting to get a little nervous herself. "Well?"

"Okay, here goes." But he took another moment before he continued. "When I first came into the station, I told you I'd had some trouble out on the road."

"I remember."

"Well, that was all true," he said. "I ran into this guy who was…having some problems. He'd pulled off the road because he wasn't feeling well. He passed out, hit his head on the bumper and when I came upon him, he was bleeding pretty badly. I drove him to a hospital in the next town, and after a little while, the doctor came out and told me that the guy hadn't made it. He had a heart attack and died. That's why he'd been feeling so poorly earlier."

"That's too bad," Grace said. "But I don't understand—"

"You will. I'm getting to the good part. The hospital needed to know how to get in touch with the guy's next of kin. I couldn't even tell them who he was. We'd just met out on the road. So, I went out to the car and opened his briefcase—this briefcase—to see if there was an address or something. That's when I found… well, take a look."

He snapped open the latches, raised the lid and stepped back.

Grace took one look inside, then shot him a look. "Are those—"

"Hardballers," he said. "Custom-made. And that's five thousand dollars in cash. And this—" He picked up the envelope. "This is what you really need to see."

A hard little knot had formed in the pit of Grace's stomach as she glanced inside the envelope, then pulled out the photograph. She read the note attached, glanced at the picture, then read the note again.

Slowly, she looked up.

"Now you know why I'm worried that the shoot-out this morning was a little more than just a warning. Someone wants you dead, Grace."

She sat down on the edge of the bed, still clutching the photograph. "You're telling me the guy who died was a hit man? Someone hired him to come here and kill me?"

"I don't have to tell you. You can see for yourself right there."

She glanced down at the photograph. It was a shot of her coming out of the station. Must have been taken right after she first got to town.

But…there was something about all this that didn't add up. Something Dale Walsh wasn't telling her.

"There's nothing in here about who I am or where I live. How did you find me?"

"Before we got to the hospital, the guy mentioned he was on his way to Jericho Pass to see someone about a job."

"Well, that's convenient," she said. "Since you were on your way here, too."

She saw him swallow before he nodded. "Exactly. I thought I'd bring the briefcase in, give it to the sheriff and hope that he would know how to find the woman in the photograph. And then I saw you."

"And you decided not to tell me? Why?"

"Because it occurred to me that I was in a unique position to find whoever had hired this guy. He probably didn't know what the hit man looked like or even what his name was. All he'd know was that sooner or later a stranger would show up in town, and I thought there was a good chance he—or she—would make contact with me. Then we'd have him."

"That is the biggest load of crap I've ever heard in my life." Grace got up and tossed the envelope toward the open briefcase. "Of all the harebrained schemes—"

"Hey," he said, looking a little wounded. "It's not that far-fetched. It could have worked."

"Why on earth didn't you just come clean with me to begin with?"

"Because for all I knew, it could have been someone close to you who hired the killer. If they got wind that he was dead, they might get desperate enough to take matters into their own hands—which is what I suspect happened today."

Grace pressed a hand to her head. "This is seriously one of the worst judgment calls I've ever heard. What were you thinking? I don't even know what to say. I'm not even sure I believe you."

"How can you not believe me?" he demanded. "The proof is right here."

Her eyes narrowed. "How do I know you're not the hit man?"

"Would I be standing here talking to you if I were?"

"Maybe, if you thought you could get away with it. What's the name of the town where the man died?" When he told her, she said, "You know I'm going to check out your story."

"That's fine. Just start taking precautions. Don't walk any place alone at night. Wear a vest. Whatever you have to do to stay safe."

"Funny that you're so concerned about my safety now."

"Believe it or not, keeping you safe has been my primary concern all along. But you're right. I made a bad judgment call. I should have come clean with you from the start."

"But you didn't, and now there's no way I can hire you. After today and now this? You're too impulsive and you seem to think you operate under a different set of rules than the rest of us. That just won't work for me. I don't trust you and I don't want you on my team."

She expected him to argue, but instead he nodded. "I screwed up. I accept that. And now I think the best thing for me to do is just get in my car and go back to where I came from."

Grace folded her arms. "I think that would be the best. And I would advise you to do so sooner rather than later, because there's still something about this story that stinks to high heaven. If I sit around thinking about it for too long, I may just decide to let you cool your jets in a holding cell while I figure it out."

CAGE GOT ALL THE WAY BACK to his room, even had the door open, before he turned and walked back to Grace's room. This time he rapped soundly, not caring who heard him.

She pulled back the door in annoyance. *"What?"*

"Just to be clear…I'm not coming to work for you. Ever."

She folded her arms.

"So there's no reason why I can't do this now."

Before she had time to protest, he bent and kissed her, threading his fingers through her hair so she couldn't pull away.

Not that she tried. Not for a moment or two at least.

What she did was part her lips and melt into the kiss. The mint toothpaste on her breath was like ambrosia, Cage thought. The floral scent of her shampoo like a summer dream. Her skin was warm, soft and inviting, and when he slid a hand down her arm to curve around her waist—

She stepped back and gave him a good slap.

Cage was stunned. He put a hand to his face. "What did you do that for?"

"You don't just come to a woman's room

and assume you'll be welcome. Next time, you ask first."

"Next time—"

She grabbed his shirt and pulled him all the way into the room. Before Cage knew it, they were kissing again and stumbling all over the place until something crashed to the floor. That stopped them for a moment, and Grace put a hand to his mouth and shushed him as she glanced over her shoulder to see what had fallen. And then they were at it again.

Cage had his arms around her as he backed her up against the wall, and one of her legs curled sensuously around his calf. They were pressed so tightly together, he couldn't have gotten to third base, let alone hit a homer, even if he'd wanted to. There was no maneuvering room, but that suited him fine for now. It was like heaven kissing her. He could go on like this all night.

When they finally broke apart, all hot and out of breath, he said, "You're not going to slap me again, are you?"

"No," she said as she tried to straighten her mussed hair. "But throwing your ass in jail is still a distinct possibility."

Chapter Fourteen

Grace's cell phone roused her from a deep sleep. She glanced at the display, saw that it was from the station, and groaned.

"Steele."

"This is Sam, Sheriff Steele. I think you better get down to the station ASAP."

"What's going on?"

"There's something here you're going to want to see."

Fifteen minutes later, she was showered, dressed and on her way out. Dale's car was still parked at the curb, so he hadn't left, but Grace hoped he'd be on his way soon. For both their sakes. He was nothing but trouble in so many ways she couldn't even begin to count them.

But he sure could kiss.

Oh, boy, could he kiss.

The man was a veritable virtuoso with his

tongue. And he had played her like a fiddle, strumming and stroking until her whole body had felt on fire, until it had been all she could do not to rip off all her clothes, throw herself on the bed and demand to know what else he could do with that tongue.

Okay, Grace, just calm down, her inner voice chided her. *It's not like you've never been kissed before.*

But it had been a long time since a first kiss had sent her to the moon and back. Too long, she realized. And now the guy that was pushing her buttons just had to be someone impulsive and undisciplined, who wouldn't know how to exercise good judgment if his life depended on it. Or worse, *her* life.

What kind of man would keep secret the fact that someone had put a hit out on her? That was information she needed to know.

That thought brought her back to earth quickly enough. Someone had put a hit out on her.

Someone had pushed her down the stairs, shot at her truck, and paid a hit man five thousand dollars up front with the promise of five thousand more when the job was finished. That was what her life was worth to someone. Just ten thousand dollars.

When she pulled up at the station, she glanced around the parking lot before she got out. Her hand rested on the handle of her gun as she hurried inside.

Sam Dickerson and Lily were waiting for her. They were both pacing in the lobby, and Lily had the strangest look on her face.

"What's going on?" Grace asked.

"Can we go into your office?"

"Sure."

She unlocked the door and they followed her inside. "What gives?"

"This was just faxed to us from Presidio County," Sam said. "Take a look."

"What is it?"

"In a nutshell? A body that was found at a rest stop off I-10 has been identified as Detective Dale Walsh of the Galveston Police Department."

CAGE WAS JUST PAST the city limits when the blue lights came on behind him. He could see the squad car in his rearview, thought that it was a Cochise County sheriff's deputy, but he had no idea why he was being pulled over.

For a split second, he entertained the notion of just flooring the accelerator and seeing what the Caddy could do out on the open road, but the deputy would undoubtedly give chase and somebody could end up hurt.

So Cage did what any law-abiding ex-cop would do. As he pulled off the road, he slipped Dale Walsh's .38 underneath the seat within easy reach, just in case.

He watched in the side mirror as the officer got out of the car. It was Grace. And she had her gun on him as she cautiously approached the car.

"Don't move," she yelled when he started to turn.

She stood several feet from the door, gun in both hands. "Get out of the car."

He did as she said. "What's going on—"

"Across the hood. Legs spread, arms behind you. Now!"

When he was spread-eagled on the hood, she kicked his feet apart, frisked him, then cuffed him.

"Do I even get to know what this is all about?" he asked when she jerked him upright.

She responded by reading him his Miranda rights. Then she led him back to the squad car, shoved him inside and slammed the door.

When she'd climbed behind the wheel, he said, "How did you know where to find me?"

"I went by Miss Nelda's. She said you'd just left."

"I thought I was getting an early start," he said with a sigh. "Get miles behind me before the sun came up."

She said nothing, just sat there staring straight ahead.

"Don't I at least get to know what I'm being arrested for?"

She turned, her eyes hard and accusing. "Who are you? And don't tell me you're Dale Walsh because he's dead. His body was found at a rest stop off I-10. And since you've taken his identity and his car, I'm assuming you must have killed him."

"No, no, no," he said a little desperately. "I didn't kill anybody. You have to believe me."

She drew a deep breath and released it. "What I believe is that everything that comes out of your mouth is a damn lie."

Leaning forward, she started the car, turned off the turret lights and U-turned back toward town.

"Grace, just listen to me, would you? I can explain everything."

"The only thing I want to know from you before we get back to the station is your name. Your *real* name."

"Cage Nichols. I'm an ex-cop from Dallas."

He saw her glance in the mirror. "*Ex*-cop?"

"Ex-SWAT to be exact. I had to leave the force about a year ago after being shot in the knee."

"What are you doing out here?"

"I sell oilfield equipment for my brother-in-law."

"And now I suppose you're going to try and tell me that you didn't have anything to do with the real Dale Walsh's death."

"I didn't, I swear it. I never even met him. The man I told you about who had the heart attack…he said *his* name was Dale Walsh. Everything I told you about him was true. We did meet out on the road. I did open that briefcase trying to find out something about his next of kin. The only difference is, I came to Jericho Pass specifically to warn you about the hit. I could have just kept going, but I didn't. I couldn't."

"You're a real noble guy, aren't you, Mr. Nichols? We'll see how noble you are when I run your prints and check out your story."

"You can't do that," he said. "You can't run my prints."

"Watch me."

"If you run my prints, I'm a dead man."

"I can't wait to hear this one," she muttered.

"YOU WANT ME TO CALL Presidio and tell 'em we got a suspect in custody?" Sam Dickerson asked eagerly.

He and Grace and Lily were all standing outside Cage's cell giving him the evil eye. They had yet to process him, but since Dale Walsh had been killed in another county, Cage would be transferred to their custody before being formally charged.

And as soon as Grace started making those calls, she'd likely bring that San Miguel mess right to her doorstep.

"Sheriff, can I talk to you for a minute?" He stood with his hands draped through the bars as he watched her watch him.

"I'm listening," she said.

"I need to talk to you alone. Please."

Grace turned to Lily and Sam. "Don't you two have something better to do than stand around gawking at a suspect?"

"Not really," Lily said with a smirk. "This is just getting too good. You never suspected a thing, Grace? All that time you two spent together? Man, that must make you feel—"

"Stupid? Gullible? Mad as hell? Yeah, pretty much," Grace said. "Does that make you feel better?"

Lily shrugged and walked out of the room.

Sam hung by the door for a minute. "Should I call Presidio or not?"

Grace shook her head. "Just hang on. I'll make the call."

Sam acted as if he didn't want to leave her alone with Cage, even though there wasn't much he could do in his present circumstances.

The deputy said from the doorway, "If he gives you any trouble, just holler." He rested his hand on the handle of his gun.

And he was itching to use it, too, Cage figured. After all, Sam was the one who'd jumped to the conclusion that Cage was Dale Walsh. He was the one who'd ushered him into the station and introduced him to Grace. In his shoes, Cage wouldn't be feeling too kindly toward him, either.

When they were alone, Grace folded her arms. "This better be good."

Cage took a breath. "It all started two days ago when my car broke down just outside of a place called San Miguel."

GRACE TRIED TO LISTEN WITH an open mind, but it was quite a story. And she had to admit, he'd done a pretty good job of motivating his questionable actions. Trouble was, she had a hard time believing anything he told her now.

To be taken in the way she had been…the way they *all* had been…

A few months earlier, Grace had read in the paper about a fourteen-year-old boy who had walked into a Chicago police station and passed himself off as a cop. He'd even partnered up with an officer and gone out on patrol for five hours. Grace had thought at the time how foolish that officer must have felt when the impersonation was finally discovered. Now that she'd experienced that same humiliation, she had a little more sympathy for the guy. It was no fun being had, and it would be a long time before she heard the last of this.

SWAT, huh? Well, that explained his cowboy attitude, she supposed. Most of the SWAT guys she'd known over the years thought pretty highly of themselves and their abilities. It would take someone with a little swagger and a lot of nerve to pull off such a scam.

"Well?" he said as he stared at her through the bars. "Aren't you going to say anything?"

"You've left me speechless," she said. "I

wouldn't have thought you could top yourself, but you've done it." She went over and stood in front of the cell door. "So you knew when you saw the dead guy yesterday morning that he was the same man you'd seen in San Miguel. And yet you didn't say a word. A connection to five murders and you keep your mouth zipped."

"And I just told you why. Those men I saw in San Miguel were cops. The minute you release my name and my description, I'm a dead man."

"Quit being so melodramatic," she said. "You're in my custody. I won't let anything happen to you."

"You won't be able to stop it. Sooner or later they'll come for me, and if you get in their way…" He gripped the bars, his gaze burning into hers. "The best thing you can do is just let me go. I'm not even asking for myself anymore. I don't want you to get caught up in this. You have enough to deal with."

"You know I can't let you go," she said.

"Then we're in big trouble, Grace."

Chapter Fifteen

The sun was just coming up over the horizon as Grace drove south, past the canyon where she and Cage—if that turned out to be his real name—had been shot at and past the site where a dead man named Sergio had been executed.

As she approached the cutoff to the Nance Ranch, she reached over and turned off the news she'd been listening to. Nothing in the broadcast about the killings in San Miguel, but that story was two days old now. There'd been more deaths along the border since then. Every new day brought more violence, Grace thought wearily, and for the first time, she began to question whether she was up for this job. Cage Nichols and all his lies had taken another bite out of her confidence.

She tried to shake it off as she pulled up in front of the house. Killing the engine, she sat there for a moment and tried to figure out how she wanted to handle the situation. She'd come out here early because she wanted to make sure she found Jesse at home and because she also wanted to catch him off guard when she showed him the copy of the deed. If his reaction was what she thought it would be—what she hoped it would be—then her instincts about him would be proven right. He'd had nothing to do with the canyon shooting, nothing to do with putting a hit out on her.

But if Jesse wasn't responsible…who was?

She squinted into the morning sun as she thought again about that shadow she'd seen at the top of the stairs, the feel of that hand on her back a split second before she tumbled down the steps. And then Lily had come in a few minutes later, not in the least surprised or concerned to hear about Grace's fall.

But her own sister? Grace refused to believe it if for no other reason than a ten thousand dollar payoff would be a little out of her sister's league.

So, who then? Who wanted her dead?

She got out of the squad car and walked up to the porch. The sky was cloudless overhead, a brilliant, seamless blue—empty except for a hawk circling nearby. The breeze out of the east was already hot and dry, and Grace could feel a trickle of sweat down her backbone as she slowly climbed the stairs.

Glancing over her shoulder, she scoured the countryside after she'd knocked. She felt uneasy and exposed all of a sudden, although she could see for miles out into the desert. There seemed to be no life at all—inside the house or out.

She knocked again, hard and fast, then opened the screen door and rapped on the glass inset. Finally, after what seemed an eternity, the door opened and Grace stood face-to-face with her ex-husband for the first time in almost fifteen years.

CAGE LAY ON HIS BACK, hands crossed behind his head as he stared up at the ceiling. The bunk mattress was hard and lumpy and probably none too clean, but he ignored the discomfort as he watched the early morning sunlight slant through the tiny window at the top of the cell. He observed the dust motes for a while, then trained his gaze on the ceiling where he counted the tiles and then the water stains.

One of the stains looked like a bird, and he thought of the thunderbird story Grace had told him the day before. And that made him think of Willow Springs and that made him think of last night.

He'd wanted badly to kiss her under the stars. Sitting with her in that old Caddy with the top down and the desert sky overhead and the smell of her perfume filling his nostrils… Cage wasn't going to lie. He'd been caught up in the moment.

And then later, when he'd kissed her in her room, it had been great. A real hot, needy, carried-away-by-lust type of kiss. But he still wanted to kiss her underneath all those stars, with the whisper of ghosts and the scent of desert wildflowers drifting on the night air. Cage had never thought of himself as a romantic, but Grace seemed to bring it out in him. Or maybe it was West Texas.

"Do you want something to eat?"

Cage bolted upright and swung his legs over the cot. He thought the woman standing on the other side of the bars was Grace at first, but then he realized it was Lily.

He got up and walked over to the door. "It's not your job to fetch breakfast, is it?"

She shrugged. "We all pitch in when and where we're needed. Most everyone else is either out on patrol or hasn't come in yet.

Since I'm already here, I thought I'd offer to get you something."

"You know what I really need?" He wrapped his hand around one of the bars. "I really need to talk to Grace."

"I doubt she's in the mood to talk to you. You kind of made a fool out of her."

"And you're enjoying every minute of it, aren't you?"

She tossed her braid over her shoulder. "If she gets a little comeuppance now and then, I'm not going to shed any tears for her."

"You don't know your sister at all," Cage said. "You've got some notion that she thinks she's perfect and infallible and above reproach, but that's not the way she sees herself. I've never seen anyone work harder for acceptance than she does."

"And you've known her, what? All of two days? I'd hardly call you an expert on my sister."

"I'm not claiming to be an expert," he said. "But I bet I've learned more about Grace in the past two days than you have in the past twenty years. She's a good person, Lily. Maybe you should think about giving her a chance."

Her mouth hardened, but Cage thought he

saw the flicker of regret in her eyes. It wasn't much, but it was something.

"Will you go tell her I want to see her?"

"I couldn't even if I wanted to. She's not here."

"Do you know when she'll be back?"

Lily shrugged. "I guess that depends on Jesse."

Cage's fingers tightened around the steel bar. "Grace went to see Jesse Nance? Why?"

"She said you guys missed him when you were out there yesterday. I guess she still wants to ask him some questions about the body that was found out by the canyon. Or maybe…" The sly smile came back. "Maybe she wants to reminisce about old times."

"Lily, you have to listen to me," Cage said.

Something in his voice must have caught her attention, because she took a step closer to the cell. "What?"

"Grace could be in big trouble. You have to get me out of here."

JESSE PUSHED THE SCREEN DOOR open and stepped out on the porch.

Grace resisted the urge to let her hand creep up to her gun where it rested in its holster. As far as she could tell, Jesse was unarmed. He was fully dressed though, even at this time of morning. Grace supposed the responsibilities of the ranch had made an early riser out of him. She could remember coming over here as a teenager and finding him still in bed at noon.

A lot of other things had changed about him, too. He was still an attractive man, but the sparkle of mischief in his eyes had hardened into a cold, brittle gleam. He looked older than his thirty-three years and a little heavier than she remembered, but the smile he flashed her was pure Jesse.

"Look at you, Gracie. All grown up and packing heat. You still know how to get a man's heart racing first thing in the morning." He leaned a shoulder against a newel post and crossed his arms, his gaze never leaving hers. "How you been?"

"Not too bad," she said. "But I'm sorry to say this isn't a social call."

"Didn't think it was," he said. "Sookie told me you stopped by yesterday. Something about a body found out by the canyon."

"You wouldn't know anything about that, would you?"

He frowned and the gleam in his eyes hardened. "You think I had something to do with that guy's death? Come on, Gracie. You know me better than that."

"I don't know you at all," she said. "Fifteen years is a long time."

"It seems like yesterday to me. We had some good times out here, didn't we? You and me and Colt. But mostly you and me." He looked her up and down, smiling. "You were something, Gracie. I never did get over you."

"Is that why you hired someone to kill me?" Grace watched him carefully. She saw surprise flash across his features, and maybe just the barest hint of anger.

"What the hell are you talking about?"

"I know about the deed, Jesse."

He sucked in a sharp breath, his gaze going from Grace out to the desert and then back again. "That was Mama's doing. I guess she didn't trust me with this place. Thought with your name on the deed you'd keep me from selling it and blowing all the money. Pretty slick of her, I guess. I didn't even know about it until after she died."

"Why didn't you tell me about it?"

His head was slightly bowed and he gazed up at her through his lashes. "Gracie. Come on. We're talking about a lot of money here."

"How much?"

"Quarter of a million. And call me crazy," he said as he straightened, "but I'm not too keen on sharing it with the woman who walked out on me."

He took a step toward her, and Grace's hand flew to the handle of her gun. "You just stay right where you are, Jesse."

His gaze dropped to the gun, then slowly raised. "Gracie, Gracie, Gracie. We've got a score to settle, you and me. And it's been a long time coming."

She heard the creak of the screen door and whirled. No one was there.

"It's just the wind, babe," Jesse said softly as he slipped up behind her.

A DUST CLOUD ROLLED over the squad car as Lily slammed the car to a halt in front of the house. She shot Cage a warning look as she reached for the door. "I don't know how I let you talk me into this, but now that we're here, I'm going to handle this my way. You just sit your ass in the car and keep your mouth shut."

"I thought you brought me out here for backup," Cage said. "Don't you think you should at least take these off?" He held up his cuffed hands.

Lily laughed. "Oh, God, is that really what you thought? I brought you out here so you could have the pleasure of witnessing Jesse and Grace's tender little reunion. If that doesn't open your eyes, I don't know what will." She climbed out of the car.

"Hey, Lily?"

She leaned down.

"It's okay to be worried about your sister. After everything I told you, you should be worried."

She gave him a dirty look. "I need my head examined, is what I need. Let me just say this. If you're conning me like you conned Grace, I will kick your sorry butt six ways to Sunday. And don't think I can't do it."

Slamming the door shut, she marched across the yard and up the porch steps to knock on the door. While she had her back to him, Cage climbed out of the car, and by the time Jesse Nance appeared in the doorway, Cage was halfway up the porch steps.

"Mornin', Jesse."

"Well, well, well, it seems to be my lot in life to be constantly sought after by beautiful women. What brings you out here, darlin'?" He opened the screen door and stepped out on the porch. His gaze lit on Cage and he took in the handcuffs with a raised brow. "This guy your prisoner, Lily?"

She shot Cage a murderous look. "Yeah, much to my sorrow."

"What'd he do?"

"What didn't he do? Stole a car, stole an identity, maybe even killed a guy."

Jesse whistled. "What's he doing out here then? What are *you* doing out here?"

"I'm looking for Grace. Have you seen her this morning?"

"This morning you say?"

"Just answer the question," Cage said.

Jesse cut his glance to Lily. "Who is this clown?"

"Answer the question, damn it. Where's Grace?"

"Why is Grace's whereabouts any business of yours?" he demanded. When Cage made a move toward him, he said, "Oh, you want a piece of this? Come on, hotshot. Bring it on."

Lily threw an arm up and gave Cage a shove in the chest as he lunged up the stairs. "Would you two just knock it off? I do not need this kind of grief. You!" She pointed a finger at Cage. "Get your butt down those steps and stay there. And *you*…" She turned on Jesse. "You tell me right now where Grace is or I might just decide to throw you two in a jail cell and let you duke it out."

Jesse was still glowering at Cage. "She was out here earlier but she left. And come to think of it, why are you asking me where she is when she left thirty minutes ago to meet you."

"Me? What makes you think that?"

"Because you called her and told her to meet you at home. At least that's what she told me."

Lily glanced down the steps at Cage. "I never called Grace."

"Well, somebody did," Jesse said. "She stood right here and told me it was you."

"If you're lying—" Lily was already punching in numbers on her cell phone. She listened for a moment, then disconnected. "She's not answering her phone."

"Let's go," Cage said. And as she hurried down the steps, he could see his own fear reflected in Lily's soft gray eyes.

Chapter Sixteen

The door was unlocked and Grace pushed it open with her toe. She drew her gun and kept it pointed downward as she eased inside. The house was cool and dim and so quiet, she could hear the thud of her own heartbeat in her ears.

Her sister's car wasn't in the driveway nor was it around back. Grace hadn't checked the barn, but she didn't think she needed to. Her sister wasn't here.

Someone had called her on her cell phone, pretending to be Lily. The call had come from inside the ranch because the number had shown up on Grace's display. But it hadn't been Lily. Grace was almost certain of that now.

Whoever was inside this house had lured Grace out here for one purpose. To trap her. She'd already called for backup, but Grace was not going to wait around and let her would-be killer get away. This was it. Time for a showdown.

She went through the bottom floor room by room, and then she climbed the stairs, pausing on the landing, just as her parents' killer had done all those years ago. Slowly she moved down the hallway, hesitating again just outside the open door to her and Lily's old bedroom.

With her gun gripped in both hands, she quickly stepped inside and swept the weapon back and forth as her gaze darted about the room, searching every nook and corner for a shadow, a movement that didn't belong.

The gauzy curtains at the window flared, and Grace realized the window was open. Had someone climbed out to the roof?

She moved over to the window and glanced out. Someone could have easily gone out that way, crept down the sloping roof, hopped onto the top of the porch and shimmied down one of the columns. Grace had done it herself as a kid.

But why go to all the trouble of getting her out here just to play this game of cat and mouse?

She moved away from the window and stood listening to the house for a moment. It was so quiet inside…

And then she heard it. The squeak of the windmill. The sound froze her in place as dread mushroomed in her chest, and for a moment, she couldn't catch her breath. Sweat trickled down her temple as she willed herself to move. To get out of that house. She recognized the beginning symptoms of a panic attack. If she didn't leave now…

She looked down at the floor where an arm had snaked out from underneath the bed. Grace jumped back, but not before the hand clamped like a vise around her ankle.

LILY HANDED CAGE the key and he managed to release himself from the cuffs while she drove like a bat out of hell down the road. "What if we don't make it in time—"

"Just drive," he said. "Don't think."

She reached down and pulled a .38 from her ankle holster. "Here," she said, and tossed it to him.

GRACE WAS YANKED off her feet and she twisted as she fell, so that she landed facedown on the hardwood floor. She broke her momentum with her hands, but her gun went flying. As she scrambled for it, the assailant slid out from the bed and in one roll was on her. Grace tried to turn and fight him off, but he clipped her on the side of the head with something hard and metal. She fell back against the floor, hand to her head, so dazed that for a moment she lost all sense of where she was.

Then slowly the stars faded and she saw Ethan Brennan standing over her with a gun. No, that couldn't be right. Ethan?

"Get up," he said. "Come on. On your feet."

As Grace struggled to rise, he grabbed her arm and yanked her up.

"What do you think you're doing?"

"Just shut up."

"This is crazy," she said. "I don't understand what you're trying to pull here."

"You don't have to understand. All you have to do is go away. Forever."

"Why?" She used her shoulder to wipe the blood from her face. "What did I ever do to you?"

"It's simple, Grace. Lily doesn't want you here."

"You're doing this for Lily?"

"Oh, don't make me sound like some love-starved geek. I'm doing this for me, too. It's something I've wanted to do for a long time. Ever since I can remember, really. I thought it might be fitting to kill you here in the same house where your parents were murdered. Symmetry and all that."

"You're not the one who called me earlier," Grace said. "Who's helping you?"

"Someone who doesn't want you here, either. But you don't need to worry about that. You don't need to worry about anything. I'll try to make it quick. Not too quick, though. Where would be the fun in that?"

Through the open window, Grace heard a car coming up the drive. Her heart surged and she saw that Ethan had heard it, too. He eased over to the window, keeping her in his line of sight as he glanced out.

"It's over," Grace said. "The police are here."

"Shut up." But a note of panic had crept into his voice. Grace waited until he glanced down at the drive again, and then she lunged. The momentum took them both through the window and as they rolled down the sloping roof, Grace grabbed for Ethan. Her hand closed around a silver medallion he wore around his neck, and she felt the cord snap as she tumbled over the side of the roof.

LILY SCREAMED when she saw Grace go over the edge of the roof, and then she spotted the silhouette of a man racing back up the slope.

It looked like…Ethan.

She and Cage were both out of the car, racing toward the house. "He went back inside," Lily said. "Go!"

When she came around the side of the house and saw Grace lying on the ground, her heart literally stopped as she dropped to her knees beside her sister.

"Grace! Can you hear me?"

Grace drew a breath and opened her eyes. "Lily?"

"Grace, are you okay? How badly are you hurt? Can you move?"

"I'm okay. I just had the wind knocked out of me."

"When I saw you go over that roof—" Lily swallowed. "I'm so sorry…"

"It's okay." Grace caught her sister's hand. "Everything will be okay, but right now we have to get some backup out here."

"We are the backup," Lily said. "Cage is inside the house with Ethan."

Chapter Seventeen

Cage found the little bastard hiding upstairs under a bed, along with a backpack filled with guns, ammo, knives, nunchakus and a garrote. Everything a do-it-yourselfer could possibly need.

It had taken very little persuasion to find out that he'd hooked up with the hired gun via an online chat room for like-minded aficionados, and that when said hired gun failed to show up at their appointed rendezvous, Ethan had decided to take matters into his own hands.

As to what happened to the real Dale Walsh, that would have to be left to speculation. Since he and the hit man had been traveling the same route, it was possible that the hit man had overheard Dale mention his destination and decided stealing another man's identity would allow him to show up in Jericho Pass without arousing suspicion. He may not even have known Walsh was a police detective.

It was also possible that Walsh had recognized the guy or otherwise caught on to him, and was shot in an ensuing confrontation. Since both principles were dead, no one would likely ever know for sure what had happened.

Cage could live with that. With the psycho geek in jail and his hired gun six feet under, a few unanswered questions was a small price to pay because Grace was safe. As safe as a sheriff in a border county could be these days.

Which brought Cage back to *his* problem. He was still a hunted man. If the bad cops weren't yet in Jericho Pass, they soon would be. It was time for him to make tracks, before they caught up with him or before Grace remembered that he was supposed to be in jail.

Still, sundown found him lingering on the steps at Miss Nelda's, waiting for Grace to show up. The fire in the sky was spectacular that evening, orange on the horizon and deep purple overhead streaked with crimson and gold.

Say what you will about the barren landscape of West Texas, Cage thought, but the sunsets couldn't be beat.

As the day melted into a soft twilight, the

air cooled and the dry wind blowing off the desert was tinged with the scent of lemon verbena from the sisters' garden and the more medicinal scent of the creosote bush that grew near the stairs.

When Grace finally drove up in her truck, she must not have seen Cage sitting there on the stairs. Or else she was trying to avoid him. She went straight inside, and a few moments later, he saw a light come on in her room. He watched her silhouette moving back and forth in front of the window, counted to ten, then rose and climbed the steps to the balcony.

She looked surprised to see him when she answered his knock, and he thought—hoped—the emotion that flickered across her face was relief.

She placed a hand on the door, the other on her hip. "I thought you'd skipped town."

"Thought about it." He folded his arms and leaned a shoulder against the frame. "Somehow it didn't seem right leaving without saying goodbye."

"Well, that's mighty brave of you," she said. "Or stupid, since by all rights, I should take you back into custody."

"I'm hoping you'll at least hear me out

before you throw the cuffs on me. Grace, look, there's something—"

"Shut up, Cage."

"What—?"

She drummed her fingers on the door facing. "I said be quiet. Every time you open your mouth, a pack of lies spills out, so maybe you just shouldn't talk for a while."

He stood there staring down at her, grinning in spite of himself because she was just so damn likable even when she wasn't.

"Well, if you don't want me to talk," he said softly, "how do you suggest we communicate?"

He barely had the words out of his mouth before she grabbed his shirt, hauled him inside, and before he knew it, she'd shoved him against the wall and planted the mother of all kisses on him.

When they finally broke apart, Cage didn't know what had hit him.

"Damn, Grace."

She was struggling with the buttons on his shirt, and he saved her the trouble by pulling it over his head and flinging it aside once he got the pesky buttoned cuffs over his hands. She was busy with her own shirt now, and Cage hopped on first one foot and then the other as he kicked off his boots. But this time, Grace was down to her underwear, and Cage felt as if someone had just flattened him with a two-by-four.

The woman had curves, he'd already known that. But to see them in all their glory…

His mouth watered to taste her beautiful breasts, and his hands itched to stroke every inch of those long, sexy legs. He was already rock hard and they were just getting started.

Grace cupped his face, pulled him down for another kiss and then when he lifted her, she wrapped her legs around his waist and they stumbled backward to the bed, sinking so deeply into the poofy featherbed that it felt a little like drowning.

Cage rolled them over too far, and they smacked the floor with a loud thud. His foot hit the desk and sent a lamp crashing against the wall, where it teetered for a moment before toppling over.

Grace, lying on her back beneath him, clapped a hand to her forehead. "There is just nothing subtle about you, is there?"

He grinned. "In about five minutes, you'll appreciate that."

"Big talker."

"Oh, I'll do more than talk," he said. "First,

I'm going to kiss you right here…" He bent and grazed his lips against the tips of her breasts. "Flick my tongue back and forth like this…"

Grace tunneled her fingers through his hair, pinning him to her as she sighed in pleasure.

"And then I'm going to run my hand up your leg, real…real…slow…until I get up to here…" He traced a finger along the edge of her panties, then slipped the fabric aside. "And here's where it starts to get good," he murmured, and the movement of his fingers brought a gasp from Grace, and then a deep, sensual moan.

He brought a finger to his lips, moistened the tip, and then touched her again, in just the right place, in just the right way, and there was nothing subtle about Grace's reaction.

She exploded like a Fourth of July rocket as Cage laughed in delight.

AFTER A WHILE, they picked themselves up off the floor, showered and dressed and sat side by side in the shadowy room with the door open, allowing the night air to drift inside as they watched the stars come out.

"This is nice," Cage said after a bit, and reached for her hand.

"It is." Grace sighed. "But you're still

leaving first thing in the morning, right? I don't want to have to throw your butt back in jail."

Cage grinned. "Why, Grace Steele, I do believe that's the nicest thing you've ever said to me."

Chapter Eighteen

The ache in Cage's knee woke him up that night. He'd put too much stress on it in the past couple of days, and now he was paying the price. He could feel the puffy tautness of the swelling, but there wasn't much he could do about that right now except to make an ice pack.

Slipping out of Grace's bed, he left her sleeping as he pulled on his jeans and boots. After putting on his shirt, he grabbed the ice bucket from the bathroom and went out the balcony door. Miss Nelda had told him that her nephew had replaced the light-bulbs, but the one near the stairs was still burned out.

Between the moon and the streetlight in front of the house, Cage could see well enough. He took his time with the stairs, favoring his good knee as much as he could, then went around the corner to the small enclosed porch where the ice machine was kept.

He'd just slid up the lid and reached for the scoop when he felt a gun barrel shoved up against the base of his head.

The ice bucket clattered to the floor as he slowly raised his arms.

"Nice and slow," a voice said behind him.

Cage turned. There were two of them, dressed much the way they had been the first time he saw them. Dark suits, white shirts. The only things missing were the shades.

The shorter of the two held him at gunpoint, while the taller man leaned a shoulder against the door. "Nice of you to accommodate us this way," he said. "It might have gotten a little messy upstairs, what with your girlfriend and all, but this way nobody has to get hurt—except you." He straightened, took a leisurely step toward Cage, and in the second before he drilled his fist into Cage's gut, bending him double, Cage caught a glimpse of the man's face.

He had the coldest eyes Cage had ever looked into.

The two men took turns pummeling him until he lay in a bloody heap on the floor. Then they grabbed him by the arms, dragged him off the porch and across the yard to the black SUV parked at the curb.

A SOUND WOKE GRACE.

She lay for a moment wondering what it was, and then she heard it again. She still couldn't place it, but she figured it was probably nothing. A cat in the yard next door. A car on the street. No reason to be alarmed. But ever since the windmill had awakened her that night all those years ago, she'd been highly attuned to nighttime noises, especially those that didn't seem to belong.

It wasn't until she sat up in bed that she realized Cage was gone. Had he slipped away in the middle of the night? That would be like him, she decided. Unpredictable and impulsive. Never a dull moment around him.

She thought of the climax she'd had earlier—the first one—and she tingled all over as she went to the door and slipped out on the balcony. Cage's car was still parked at the curb, so he hadn't left yet. Maybe he'd gone out for a walk.

As she hurried to the stairs, a tiny piece of glass dug into her foot. She leaned against the wall, balancing on one leg as she tried to pick out the splinter. Then she saw the tiny shards glistening all over the balcony where someone had broken a glass. But in the next instant, she realized that the milky-like slivers were from the overhead light. The bulb had shattered. With shoes or boots, the miniscule pieces would have gone unnoticed, but they were treacherous on bare feet. The larger chunks must have been swept away, Grace thought.

Walking on her heel, she moved to the top of the stairs, then paused when she spotted someone moving about below her. She thought at first it was Cage, and then she saw the shadows separate and realized that it was two men. No, three. The third was being dragged unconscious to the curb where a black SUV waited. A door opened, and the lifeless figure was shoved into the back. One man climbed in behind the wheel, the taller of the two strode to the other side. As he opened the door, his gaze lifted and Grace jerked back, flattening herself against the wall, praying that she was hidden by shadows.

For the longest time, the tall man scoured the darkness. Finally, he climbed in and the SUV glided away from the curb.

IT HAD TAKEN GRACE less than a minute to hurry back to her room, grab shoes, clothes and her gun and then she was running down the stairs and across the yard to her truck, cell phone to her ear as she called for backup. The roar of the wind through the back window was a graphic reminder of the close call she and Cage had had the day before. But now *he* was the target. He was in grave danger—if he was even still alive—and unless Grace could pick up the SUV's trail—

There it was, three blocks ahead of her and turning right, onto the highway. This time of night, the road was deserted. Grace spotted the huge vehicle easily, but the trick was to keep them from seeing her.

Once on the highway, she ran without lights, hanging back as far as she dared. Up ahead, the SUV lights cut off suddenly, and Grace reduced her speed, not wanting to run up on them. After a few minutes, she began to think she might have lost them, but then she saw the lights flash up ahead and off to the right. The driver had turned off the highway onto the trail that led back through the rocky terrain to Willow Springs.

Even in her truck, Grace knew she couldn't make it. She didn't know how long it would be before she had to take to the trail on foot. But to her amazement, the ruts smoothed out after a couple of miles, and she realized the road had been recently graded. Someone must have been using this trail for some time now.

She stopped and cut the engine. The windows were all down, and she could hear the faint hum of the SUV, and a moment later, the thud of tires as they crossed the old wooden bridge. If a vehicle that heavy could make it across, so could she.

Grace pressed the accelerator and her truck shot forward.

WHEN CAGE CAME TO, he found himself in the middle of a dirt road, surrounded by dilapidated buildings. He'd been lying on his side where he'd obviously been dumped, but when he groaned, hands grabbed him, pulled him to his knees, and tied his wrists behind him.

There were three other men in the road beside him, all in the same position as he. All, no doubt, with the same cold feeling of horror and dread and disbelief as they closed their eyes and awaited their execution.

The other three were members of a rival drug cartel, from what Cage could gather.

His kidnappers, ex-DEA agents, apparently worked for the highest bidder.

The man with the cold eyes walked to the end of the line, put the gun barrel to the back of a dark head, and fired.

The victim pitched forward—dead before he even hit the ground.

A QUARTER OF A MILE from the ghost town, Grace had abandoned her truck. It was so quiet out here, someone would surely hear the engine if she drove any farther.

She was fully dressed now, including boots and her gun belt, which she buckled around her as she moved as quickly as she dared toward the tumbledown buildings of the ghost town.

It had been years since she'd been out to Willow Springs. There wasn't much left. Just a few decrepit shacks and a graveyard of rusted-out vehicles. Grace could hear voices just ahead, and flattening herself to the rotting walls of one of the buildings, she peered around the corner.

What she saw nearly stopped her heart.

Pressing herself against the flimsy boards, she closed her eyes and braced for what was about to come, for what she had to do. She gripped the handle of her gun, took another breath and then a voice said from inside the building, "You just hold it right there."

Sookie stepped through the sagging doorway with a .45 trained on Grace. "I didn't want it to come to this, but it looks like if I want you dead, I'm going to have to do it myself. Should have known better than to send a boy to do a woman's job."

"You mean Ethan?"

"'I know a hit man,'" she mimicked. "'You want Grace dead? *No problem.*'" She rolled her eyes as she took another step toward Grace. "Now I ask you? What kind of idiot hires a hit man over the Internet, sight unseen, no references, no credentials, no nothing. God, what a doofus. Now, he'll be sweating it out in Huntsville for the next ten to twenty. Like I said, don't send a boy to do a woman's job. Ain't that right, sugar?" she called over her shoulder. "Just throw your gun over here. Let's not draw this out any longer than we have."

"Better do as she says, Gracie," Colt said as he came up behind Sookie.

For the longest moment, Grace's gaze held his in disbelief. Then she got mad. "You son of a bitch. Why are you doing this?"

He shrugged. "Money. Excitement. Does it matter?"

"Rescuing wild horses, my ass," she said. "You want Jesse's ranch because of its proximity to the border. I'm guessing you've already been using it for quite some time now. What happened? Did Jesse want out?"

Sookie laughed. "Poor Jesse's still living in a dream world. I think he's still got a thing for you, Grace. You know what he thought? He thought he could just show you that deed and you'd sign over your share without blinking an eye. But you and me, we're realists aren't we? You said it yourself, we have a lot in common. We might even be friends if, you know, I didn't have to kill you and all. And I still need you to toss that weapon over here."

"Do as she says, Grace. You can't shoot us both. The moment you fire that gun, those guys will be all over you." He nodded toward the street. "And trust me, you don't want to die that way."

"Just tell me one thing. Why did you want me to come back here?" When Colt merely smiled, she said, "I see. You don't have much faith in my ability, do you?"

"Your reputation in Austin preceded you.

It's a shame, really. You once had so much potential. But now…I'm afraid it's come to this. So toss down the gun and let's get this over with."

Grace made sure to throw the weapon at Sookie's feet, out of Colt's reach. When Sookie bent to pick it up, Grace pulled a .38 from the back of her jeans and fired twice.

AT THE SOUND OF GUNFIRE, all hell broke loose. Suddenly, the execution was in complete disarray.

Cage swung around and lunged at his would-be killer. They both went down, fighting like mad dogs in the dirt.

He got his hands around the man's throat and dug his thumbs into the windpipe. Out of the corner of his eye, he saw a second guy bearing down on him. The man smiled, took aim, then dropped to his knees as a .45 slug caught him square in the chest.

Bullets riddled the air. Cage thought the cavalry must have arrived, but he would later learn it was just Grace, mad as hell and armed with both a .38 and a .45.

He was still battling it out with the cold-eyed man in the dirt. And losing ground. The man tore Cage's hands from his throat, heaved him aside, and then somehow managed to get a foot in Cage's groin to send him sprawling.

And that was all the time the man needed.

He dove for his gun.

Cage heard his name, saw Grace moving up rapidly, still exchanging fire with someone holed up in one of the buildings. She screamed his name again, tossed him the .38 and Cage pulled the trigger as the cold-eyed man turned. He got off a round, grazing Cage's arm, but the second bullet took the guy down for good.

A moment later, there was nothing but silence.

Dead silence.

Whether the man in the building had been hit or was on the run, Cage didn't much care at the moment. He struggled to his feet, clutching his arm as Grace ran over to him.

And there, in the middle of a ghost town, with the smell of gunpowder perfuming the night air, Cage finally kissed Grace beneath a blanket of stars.

Chapter Nineteen

Grace's office had soon been overrun with agents from the DEA, the FBI, the TBI and maybe even a Texas ranger or two. Cage had lost count of how many times he'd had to tell his story. The legalities would likely take weeks to sort out, but he wasn't up to worrying about any of that just now. He had his arm patched up and enough painkillers to stabilize an elephant. He felt like a new man.

Grace had finally managed to tear herself away from all the red tape, and she, Lily and Cage had met up at the diner to hash everything out amongst themselves.

Lily was beside herself with guilt. "I'm so sorry, Grace." She must have said it a million times by now.

And Grace's response was always the same. "It's not your fault. You didn't cause Ethan to go off the deep end like that."

"But maybe I did. If I hadn't acted the way I did toward you, he never would have gotten the idea to try and kill you. He did that for me."

"No, he didn't. He did it for his own sick, selfish reasons," Grace said. "You had nothing to do with it. And besides, if you hadn't had the good sense to listen to Cage here—" He threw her a sheepish grin. "I'd be dead by now. You two saved my life, and I'll never forget it."

"There's a lot I want to say to you," Lily said.

Grace smiled. "There's a lot I want to say to you, too. But we've got plenty of time."

Unlike us, Cage thought.

After Lily left, he and Grace walked across the street to Miss Nelda's and sat down on the steps.

"So, what's going to happen now?" she said.

He shrugged. "I guess at some point I'll either have to give a deposition or testify, depending on how everything gets sorted out. After that…"

"Where will you go when you leave here?"

He looked out over the street where the sun baked down from a cloudless blue sky. "Maybe go on to El Paso and see if I can salvage the equipment deal for my brother-in-law. After that, back to Dallas, I guess."

"Will I ever see you again?"

He turned and studied her for a long moment. She had cuts and scratches all over her face and dark circles of exhaustion underneath her eyes. She looked like hell and Cage had never been more attracted to her.

"I'm not big on making long-term plans," he finally said.

"I kind of figured."

"But I've had in mind for some time now that I might like to get back in the game."

"Football?" she asked in disbelief.

"No, but thanks for your vote of confidence," he said with a grin. "Law enforcement. Although I could never pass the physical to be on a police force again, I was thinking I might like to open up a P.I. shop, something like that."

Grace thought about it for a minute. "Whereabouts do you have in mind? Dallas?"

"I don't know. Maybe someplace out west," he said. "I've kind of grown partial to the scenery out here." He gave her another quick once-over and a grin.

"Yeah, me, too."

"So here's what I'm thinking. You asked if we'd ever see each other again. The truth is, I don't know. I don't know where I'll be tomorrow, much less a year from now. And I don't know if what I'm feeling at this moment is even real. We've only known each other for what…thirty-six hours? And getting shot at for about half that time kind of screws with your perspective."

"No kidding," she said dryly, but he could see a curious, hopeful spark in her eyes.

"What I do know is this…I don't want to look back five years from now and wonder if I let the best thing that ever happened to me get away."

She took a deep breath and smiled. "What do we do?"

He put his hand on her knee and squeezed. "I'll tell you exactly what we'll do. I'm going off to start my business and you're going to finish the job you started here in Jericho Pass. And then in six months…oh, what the hell, let's make it three…we meet right back here, on these steps, and see where we want to go from there."

"Sounds kind of cheesy, but I like it," Grace said. "Three months is a long time, though. Anything can happen."

"Don't I know it," Cage said. His football dreams had died in a heartbeat, and so had his career as a cop. And in just the space of a few short days, he'd fallen in love for the first time in his life. Despite what he'd told her, he didn't need three months to know how he felt about Grace. He didn't even need three days. But she did. She was the kind of woman who needed to take her time, and Cage could live with that. He wanted her to be sure.

"What are you thinking about?" she asked.

"I was just thinking about what a lucky guy I am," he said softly.

"Just wait until we get upstairs," she said. "You're about to get even luckier."

And he did.

* * * * *

*Celebrate 60 years of pure reading
pleasure with Harlequin!*

To commemorate the event, Harlequin
Intrigue® is thrilled to invite you to the
wedding of The Colby Agency's J. T.
Baxley and his bride, Eve Mattson.

That is, of course, if J.T. can find the
woman who left him at the altar. Considering he's a private investigator for one of
the top agencies in the country—the best
of the best—that shouldn't be a problem.
The real setback is that his bride isn't
who she appears to be…and her mysterious past has put them both in danger.

*Enjoy an exclusive glimpse of
Debra Webb's latest addition to*
THE COLBY AGENCY:
ELITE RECONNAISSANCE DIVISION

THE BRIDE'S SECRETS

*Available August 2009
from Harlequin Intrigue®.*

The dark figures on the dock were still firing. The bullets cutting through the surface of the water without the warning boom of shots told Eve they were using silencers.

That was to her benefit. Silencers decreased the accuracy of every shot and lessened the range.

She grabbed for the rocks. Scrambled through the darkness. Bumped her knee on a boulder. Cursed.

Burrowing into the waist-deep grass, she kept low and crawled forward. Faster. Pushed harder. Needed as much distance as possible.

Shots pinged on the rocks.

J.T. scrambled alongside her.

He was breathing hard.

They had to stay close to the ground until they reached the next row of warehouses. Even though she was relatively certain they were out of range at this point, she wasn't taking any risks. And she wasn't slowing down.

J.T. had to keep up.

The splat of a bullet hitting the ground next to Eve had her rolling left. Maybe they weren't completely out of range.

She bumped J.T. He grunted.

His injured arm. Dammit. She could apologize later.

Half a dozen more yards.

Almost in the clear.

As she reached the cover of the alley between the first two warehouses she tensed.

Silence.

No pings or splats.

She glanced back at the dock. Deserted.

Time to run.

Her car was parked another block down.

Pushing to her feet, she sprinted forward. The wet bag dragged at her shoulder. She ignored it.

By the time she reached the lot where her car was parked, she had dug the keys from her pocket and hit the fob. Six seconds later she was behind the wheel. She hit the ignition as J.T. collapsed into the passenger seat. Tires squealed as she spun out of the slot.

"What the hell did you do to me?"

From the corner of her eye she watched him shake his head in an attempt to clear it.

He would be pissed when she told him about the tranquilizer.

She'd needed him cooperative until she formulated a plan. A drug-induced state of unconsciousness had been the fastest and most efficient method to ensure his continued solidarity.

"I can't really talk right now." Eve weaved into the right lane as the street widened to four lanes. What she needed was traffic. It was Saturday night—shouldn't be that difficult to find as soon as they were out of the old warehouse district.

A glance in the rearview mirror warned that their unwanted company had caught up.

Sensing her tension, J.T. turned to peer over his left shoulder.

"I hope you have a plan B."

She shot him a look. "There's always plan G." Then she pulled the Glock out of her waistband.

Cutting the steering wheel left, she slid between two vehicles. Another veer to the right and she'd put several cars between hers and the enemy.

She was betting they wouldn't pull out the

firepower in the open like this, but a girl could never be too sure when it came to an unknown enemy.

Deep blending was the way to go.

Two traffic lights ahead the marquee of a movie theater provided exactly the opportunity she was looking for.

The digital numbers on the dash indicated it was just past midnight. Perfect timing. The late movie would be purging its audience into the crowd of teenagers who liked hanging out in the parking lot.

She took a hard right onto the property that sported a twelve-screen theater, numerous fast-food hot spots and a chain superstore. Speeding across the lot, she selected a lane of parking slots. Pulling in as close to the theater entrance as possible, she shut off the engine and reached for her door.

"Let's go."

Thankfully he didn't argue.

Rounding the hood of her car, she shoved the Glock into her bag, then wrapped her arm around J.T.'s and merged into the crowd.

With her free hand she finger-combed her long hair. It was soaked, as were her clothes. The kids she bumped into noticed, gave her death-ray glares.

They just didn't know.

As she and J.T. moved in closer to the building, she grabbed a baseball cap from an innocent bystander. The crowd made it easy. The kid who owned the cap had made it even easier by stuffing the cap bill-first into his waistband at the small of his back.

Pushing through the loitering crowd, she made her way to the side of the building next to the main entrance. She pushed J.T. against the wall and dropped her bag to the ground. Peeled off her T-shirt and let it fall.

His gaze instantly zeroed in on her breasts, where the cami she wore had glued to her skin like an extra layer. A zing of desire shot through her veins.

Not the time.

With a flick of her wrist she twisted her hair up and clamped the cap atop the blond mass.

"They're coming," J.T. muttered as he gazed at some point beyond her.

"Yeah, I know." She planted her palms against the wall on either side of him and leaned in. "Keep your eyes open. Let me know when they're inside."

Then she planted her lips on his.

* * * * *

Will J.T. and Eve be caught in the moment?
Or will Eve get the chance to reveal
all of her secrets?
Find out in
THE BRIDE'S SECRETS
by Debra Webb
Available August 2009
from Harlequin Intrigue®.

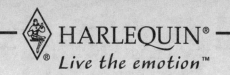

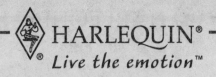

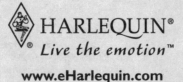

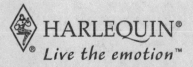

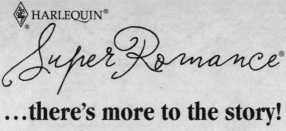
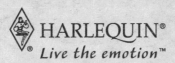

Harlequin® Historical
Historical Romantic Adventure!

*Imagine a time of chivalrous
knights and unconventional ladies,
roguish rakes and impetuous
heiresses, rugged cowboys
and spirited frontierswomen—
these rich and vivid tales will
capture your imagination!*

*Harlequin Historical . . .
they're too good to miss!*